About Tania Joyce

Tania Joyce is an Australian author of contemporary and new adult romance novels. Her stories thread romance, drama and passion into beautiful locations ranging from the dazzling lights and glitter of New York, to the rural countryside of the Hunter Valley.

She's widely traveled, has a diverse background in the corporate world and has a love for sparkles, shoes and shiraz.

Tania draws on her real-life experiences and combines them with her *very* vivid imagination to form the foundation of her novels. She likes to write about strong-minded, career-oriented heroes and heroines that go through drama-filled hell, have steamy encounters and risk everything as they endeavor to find their happy-ever-after.

Tania shuffles the hours in her day between part-time work, family life and writing. One day she hopes to find balance!

Visit www.taniajoyce.com

Dangerous Acquisitions

Strictly Business – Book 2

by

Tania Joyce

For lovers of wine.

Prologue

Two years after Tempting Propositions
June

"Damn it."

Troy cursed as steam shot out of the coffee machine nozzle and milk exploded all over the counter. His hands shook uncontrollably as he placed the pitcher of scalded milk on the counter and looked around for a cloth to clean up the mess. He was no professional barista, but he could make a cup of coffee when needed without this chaos. As he wiped the bench, his mind was elsewhere. Why did his boss, Nick Hill, want to meet with him? Had something happened in the vineyard that he had overlooked?

As he cleaned up and made a fresh brew, the knot in his stomach grew worse. Nick had sounded so formal on the phone when he called earlier for Troy to come up to the office for a meeting. Troy had worked for nearly three years at Gumtrees

Winery and didn't think anything was wrong. But his damned right knee was aching profusely, making him draw unfavorable conclusions. Like a sixth sense, his knee only played up in times of change. And at thirty-nine years of age, he'd had enough of those to last him a lifetime. What was in store for him now? He bent and wriggled his knee around to try to ward off the uneasy feeling. Unable to delay any longer, he grabbed his coffee and walked out through the glass door onto the restaurant terrace. Nick stood up from behind one of the tables and greeted him with a smile. But when Troy shook Nick's clammy hand, his concern jumped up another notch. Something wasn't right.

"Sorry to pull you up here when we're so busy out in the field, but there's something I need to talk to you about. Please, grab a seat." Nick pointed to the chair across from him as he sat down.

"Is everything okay?" Troy asked, eyeing the pile of manila folders bulging with documents resting on the table. He'd become good friends with Nick over the past few years, and seeing the tension creasing Nick's brow, he could tell something was on his mind.

Before Nick could reply, Maria, his wife, joined them and took a seat by his side. Troy shuffled around on his chair trying to get comfortable but was unable to stop his legs from jittering underneath the table. The two owners had never summonsed him to a meeting like this before. "Are you sure there's nothing wrong?"

Nick rubbed the side of his unshaven cheek. "No. No. Nothing's wrong. Quite the opposite, actually. I've been up half the night trying to come up with a good spiel to give to you, but you know me, I'm no good at bullshitting. We want to run something past you." He glanced sideways at Maria, who gave him a quick smile and a nod. "We've finalized our business plan to expand Gumtrees to include a new functions room, a few new cabins, and have documented some ideas on increasing our vineyard production, sales and capacity. Maria's restaurant is becoming more popular and we want to take advantage of the growing demand for weddings and larger functions. Sales are good and the vineyard production is up." He grinned, crow's-feet etched at the corner of his eyes.

Troy nodded, listened intently, but wondered where this was leading.

"You've been a big part of that. Your knowledge and viticulture skills surpass most people I've known in this industry for years. We'd hate to lose you to some other grower in the area—"

"I've got no intentions of going anywhere, if that's what you're afraid of." Troy butted in, wanting to assure them of his loyalty.

Nick placed his hands, palms faced down, on the table. "That's good to know, because we have a proposal for you." He pulled his shoulders back, straightening in his chair. "We were wondering ... if you'd be interested in becoming a business partner with us. Buy in and invest into the future of Gumtrees."

Troy's mouth fell open as he held his cup suspended in midair, halfway between his lips and the table. "Are you serious?"

"Absolutely." Maria added. "You've done more for this place in the past few years than we've done in twenty. We don't know whether it's because you spend all that time talking to the vines, but the vineyard is performing beyond our expectations. You're great with the guests and you help out with running the place. You don't mind changing dirty linen for me when I need help. You've become part of the landscape around here and we'd like to keep it that way."

"Wow!" Troy leaned back in his chair as all the breath in his lungs escaped with a gush. His mind wheeled around in circles as he tried to make sense of what was being said.

"I don't know if you have the financial means to do so," Nick said, "but Maria and I have met with our accountant and thought it would be a great opportunity for all of us. I've had them draw up this proposal and put it with our business plan for you to review." Nick handed him the manila folder and all of its contents across the table. Troy opened it and flicked through the pages, not taking any real notice of the words or figures flashing before him. "Have a look through it and let us know if there is anything you want to discuss. You know our turnover. You know our expenses. And you know we're growing. Maria and I think you're a critical part of our success and want you to be a part of our future."

Troy stared at the folder as his chest swelled. Relief surged through his veins. Becoming a business partner was one scenario he'd never contemplated.

Leaving the United States and the death of his wife, Nicola, behind him, being able to do something he loved every day gave him purpose. Coming back to the Hunter Valley after twenty years of absence had astounded him, delivering one surprise after another. First, he found work here. Second, he found out he had a grown son, Conner. Third, he'd rekindled old friendships. Some not as well as he would've liked. And now Nick and Maria wanted him to become a partner.

Troy put the folder down and wiped his hand down across his face. There was so much to consider. Money—that shouldn't be an issue, he had a handsome sum stowed away. Nicola's life insurance payout, his savings and his small inheritance had never been touched. Grounding—was it time he had stability again and put his roots down, like those fifty-year-old grapevines in the front paddock? Reality—he loved this place, but this decision would impact the rest of his life. He was content with the way things were. Buying in was such a huge commitment. He was a viticulturist and left the business side of things up to others. He glanced between the two of them as he toyed with the idea. "I'm honored you think so highly of me. Thank you. For a moment there, I thought you were going to sack me."

Nick laughed. "Hell no. Sorry to have caused you concern."

"When do you need an answer?"

"Is one or two weeks long enough?"

"I'll have an answer for you in one."

Troy's shoulders relaxed as he looked out over the rolling hills covered in grapevines toward the Brokenback Mountains that flanked the Valley in the distance. He had never been one to make plans or set goals or have any real driving ambition. Maybe it was time he did. Was this the opportunity he had to take? Life had dealt him enough blows, maybe it was time something went his way.

Chapter 1

January–Six Months Later

"That's the last one." Kelleigh Johnstone hoisted the final cardboard box on to the top of the others piled high in the back of her sister's garage. As she wiped her sweaty hands on the backside of her shorts, she couldn't believe her entire life was packed away into a measly half a dozen large storage boxes.

"Thank goodness," Francesca wiped her brow. Kelleigh could see her sister struggled in the heat inflicted on them thanks to the brutal, energy-sucking heatwave unleashing itself over Melbourne. Fran shouldn't be working so hard in her pregnant condition but had insisted on helping Kelleigh move the last of her belongings out of her apartment. "Let's go and grab a cold drink."

Kelleigh followed Fran into the small kitchen and sat down at the table. Placing her elbows on the surface and leaning forward, she rubbed her fingers into her temples to relieve the tension while her sister fetched cool drinks of iced water.

"I can't thank you enough for this, sis," Kelleigh said. "It won't be for long. I promise. After this work trip, I'll find somewhere to live and then clear all my stuff out." She swirled the ice around in her glass. Who was she kidding? Where would she be able to find somewhere affordable in the inner city of Melbourne? She barely had enough money to buy food, let alone pay rent.

Fran sat down at the table; her growing baby belly nudged the edge. "There's no rush. It can stay here for as long as you need. It's the least I can do to help you. I wish I had the money to loan you, but with my income, a mortgage and bills to pay, I've nothing spare."

Kelleigh reached across the table and squeezed Fran's hand. "No. No. You've done so much for me already by letting me crash on your floor for the past few days while I've moved out of my apartment, and now letting me store my stuff here."

Yes, she was in a world of hurt, but at least her problems didn't affect anyone else. No one was relying on her. With Fran's boyfriend out of work and a baby due in two months, Kelleigh wished she could do more to repay her sister. She leaned forward and knocked her forehead several times on the wooden surface of the table. "I'm sorry, Fran. I can't believe this has happened to me." She sat back up with a rush to her head and stared at nothing in particular on the ceiling. "I thought I was an intelligent woman. How could I have been so naïve?" Numbness still consumed her. The shock the life she knew was over still clouded her mind. "I've wasted five years of my life with someone I thought loved me. How could Rodrigo have done this to me? He's left me with nothing. Absolutely nothing. No. Wait. Yes, he did. He left me with a humungous debt that is going to take me a lifetime to pay off."

Fran tilted her head, her eyes washed over with sympathy. "Rodrigo had everyone fooled. Don't be so hard on yourself. Karma's going to have fun with him when his turn comes around."

That did make her feel a smidgen better. She hoped she was there to watch. If only she could track him down. Four weeks ago, while she was at work, the asshole had disappeared from her life with nearly the entire contents of her apartment and his car. Leaving her with nothing.

How stupid had she been to trust him with their finances? She'd believed in his goals and dreams and supported his ventures, that's what you did when you committed to a relationship and lived together. But no. Rodrigo, her tall, dark and handsome man, was nothing but a sham and a fraud. His car audio shop had gone bankrupt, he'd left a debtors' list behind him as long as his arm, he'd maxed out her credit cards and had taken out every last cent in their bank account.

"You know what?" Fran said. "This work trip is just what you need. A month away from all your problems will help you clear your head. You're not the first one to be scammed by their partner. You've done all you can and now it's up to the police and lawyers to find him. Life with Rodrigo is over, get over it. It's time to start anew."

Kelleigh glared at Fran across the table. She hated it when Fran was right, and she did need to start focusing on the positives. She had a good job, she had her sister ... and she wasn't pregnant. She shuddered at the thought; definitely grateful not to be carrying Rodrigo's child. But the very thought of starting again at thirty-three years of age seemed like such a daunting task. It wasn't until everything was gone that she realized she'd been living in a bubble for so long, and Rodrigo had controlled every aspect of her life.

With a sigh, Kelleigh's shoulders relaxed and she directed a heartwarming smile toward Fran. Her sister had been her strength, dragging her around to endless meetings with police, lawyers and the banks over the past few weeks. How could she ever thank her?

Kelleigh jumped when the door banged open. Jamie walked in, tugging his tie loose. He walked over and gave Fran a kiss on the cheek.

"How'd the interview go, babe?" Fran asked, her eyes full of hope.

"Not good. I didn't have enough customer service experience for their liking," he said as he flopped onto the chair beside Fran and took her hand in his. "So much for catching up with the owner on a Sunday. It's okay, I have another two interviews tomorrow. Everything's going to be fine."

Jamie looked at Fran with a sparkle in his eye and rested his hand upon her belly. "How's bubby doing today?" His voice softened as he nudged in closer to her. "Can I get you anything?"

A twinging ache flared in Kelleigh's chest as she watched her sister and Jamie adore each other. Feeling like an intruder, she shuffled around uncomfortably on her chair. Rodrigo had never looked at her like that. Never swooned at her like that. It was definitely a good thing he was gone. If she ever started dating again in the future, she made a mental note to ensure that her new man must look at her the way Jamie looked at Fran.

Kelleigh cleared her throat loudly and slid the chair back from the table. "It's nearly lunchtime; I'd better get going; I've a big ten hour drive ahead of me. I don't want to get into Sydney too late on a Sunday night. Then, tomorrow morning, I'll head straight out to the Hunter Valley. The area of Pokolbin is only about a two or so hour drive from the city; I'll be there in time for my meeting at eleven o'clock." Kelleigh picked up her bag to leave and headed for the door.

Fran and Jamie followed her out to the car. Hot sunshine blazed against her face. Kelleigh turned and wrapped her arms around her sister, held her tight, and squeezed. "Thank you for everything. I wouldn't have made it through these past few weeks without you. You're the best. You take care of yourself and bubby. I'll call you when I get to the hotel tomorrow."

Reluctantly Kelleigh let go of Fran, kissed Jamie goodbye on the cheek. She opened the car door and got in. She hated this car, but it was the only thing left to her name. It was one thing Rodrigo hadn't gotten his hands on. But, like everything else, it had to be sold to help pay off her debts. She wouldn't miss the ugly electric blue coupe at all when she returned to Melbourne after this project. She grimaced as she turned the key and the loud turbo engine roared to life and the air conditioning blasted into her face. "Come on, you ugly heap of metal. Let's get to Sydney!"

Chapter 2

The dirt road was heavily corrugated and still in desperate need of repair after the long-forgotten spring rains. Troy Smith lurched from side to side as his Landcruiser bounced over the divots on his way past Gumtree's vineyard. With each bump his knee ached profusely. Almost throbbing uncontrollably. With one free hand he rubbed and massaged his kneecap, hoping it was the rough road causing him grief, and not his intuition.

Keeping an eye on the fence line as he drove along, he peered up toward the endless blue sky; Troy noticed the hot summer's day was getting away from him. His neighbor Larry Peterson's steers had broken out of their paddock last night and made a downright mess among some of the vineyard's trellises. Troy's plans for working in the field today had to be put on hold after spending most of the morning getting the animals back into their rightful place. Now he had to find Jett, Larry's farmhand, to fix the broken fence and prevent the cattle from getting back in among the semillon vines.

As his Landcruiser crawled over the top of the hill, Troy's attention was drawn to a bright blue car a hundred meters ahead of him, stuck on the side of the road, angled precariously in the steep ditch. A Mini Coupe! He chuckled at the stupidity of the driver. Of all things to be driving on a dirt road. It was probably some young kid hooning around pretending to be a rally driver. Deep scrape marks had embedded tracks into the road's rough surface. *Idiots.*

As he drove closer, his eyes widened when he saw a woman walk around from the front of the car. City folk. Definitely not from around here. He shook his head when she nearly lost her balance, her high-heeled stilettos wiggling on the rocks. Her professional attire of white blouse and black pants wasn't going to stay clean for long against all the dust and grease as she squatted down and attempted to undo the nuts of the car tire. He sighed. He couldn't leave her stranded out here in this heat, so he pulled up on the road across from her and hopped out.

"Would you like some help with that?" he asked, waiting for the woman to acknowledge his existence.

She stood up straight with her back to him, wielding the tire wrench in her hand with an excessively tight grip. He heard her inhale deeply before swinging around to face him. Troy stopped still as he laid eyes on her. His knees buckled beneath him and he had to take a step back to regain his balance. Was it the heat of the day playing tricks on him, a mirage? He stayed motionless as she glared at him with stunning emerald green eyes. *Please help me, God!* With raven-black hair falling loosely across her shoulders and flawless skin shining golden in the sun, she had an uncanny resemblance to Nicola, his deceased wife.

His mouth fell open, unable to form any words as his heart lurched in his chest.

"Thank you, but I'm perfectly capable of changing a car tire," she said through a tensed jawline, pointing the bar in his direction.

With that, she turned back to the car, placed the head of the wrench on the nut of the tire and tried to turn it.

Blinking, he took hold of his senses. Silly nonsense. He must need food or something; maybe his blood sugar was low, making his mind play tricks on him. She looked nothing like Nicola. Taller. Slimmer. A momentary lapse, that's all.

She continued to struggle, and he wondered how long it would be before she accepted his offer. Waiting patiently, he leaned back against the side of his car, crossed his arms and ankles and watched, amused by her futile attempts to loosen the nuts. He smiled when a guttural groan came from her throat as she channeled all her energy and force against the bar; it failed to move an inch.

"Are you sure you don't need any help?" he questioned again, keeping a cautious eye on the bar in her hands. "You're going to get your clothes all ruined." He glanced over her slender frame, noting she wasn't one of those designer-label types, like Jessica, but still totally out of place. The clothes. The coupe car. The attitude.

"I'm fine!" she said as she strained on the tool with all her might.

"Okay then." Troy said, turning to get back in his car. Not that he had any intention of leaving her stranded here in the middle of nowhere.

"No wait!" came a soft pleading voice. "I'm sorry. If you don't mind, I could do with a hand. I can't seem to loosen any of the nuts." From the distraught look on her face, defeat had taken its toll.

Troy raised an eyebrow as he approached her. "What makes you think I'll do any better?" he said as he took the tool from her hand.

"Well ..."

Color rose in his cheeks as he saw her eyes scan his body, over his arms and torso and back up to his face. Tingles crawled across his skin as she assessed him up and down. "You do look a little stronger than me." She said stepping away from the wheel.

Kneeling down in front of the tire, he placed the bar into position and pried the first nut off with little effort. *Thank God!* He sighed with relief. Grateful that the nut released and he wasn't made to look a fool in front of this damsel in distress.

As he undid the third nut, he paused and wrinkled his nose. He smelt oil … and fuel. Dropping down onto his side to lie on the dirt, he peered up underneath the car. He didn't like what he saw. Oil sump punctured. Black liquid trickled out and pooled all over the ground. Axle bent. Muffler broken and a whole lot of other damage he could add to the list.

He stood up and dusted his hands off on his jeans. "I don't think changing your tire is going to help much. You won't be driving this thing anywhere. Just how far did you drive with the tire blown?" He glanced back along the road and saw the scrape marks went for about fifty meters and grimaced. "The entire underbody is cactus." As he listed off the damage, he watched her face pale in horror.

"Goddamn it!" She cursed and punched her fists into the air. With force she kicked at the rocks on the road in her high-heeled shoes. Troy could understand her frustrations. He stood still, watching her outburst as she continued to abuse nothing in particular. She stormed back over to her car, bent down on her knees and looked underneath. After assessing the damage, she stood back up and kicked the tire again and again. "This is not what I need right now, you useless heap of junk!"

Troy rubbed at the back of his neck. *Someone was having a bad day.* "It's okay. I'll help you. Are you a member of the NRMA Roadside Assistance? If you like I can call Dennis for you; he's one of the local reps who'll be able to tow this into the workshop in Cessnock."

"Thanks, but I can call them." She yanked open the car door, ripped open the glove box and searched in the car's documentation folders for the number. She stopped and dropped her face into her hands. A moment later she walked over to him and held out the book with trembling hands. "Which number do I call?"

Troy wiped away the sweat starting to accumulate on his brow in the heat of the midday sun. He scanned down the list of numbers and found the correct one. As she dialed the number and spoke on the phone, her voice chimed regardless of her constant cursing and swearing. She held him intrigued as she glared at her watch or thumped the bonnet of her car with brute force with her clenched hand. She sure was a feisty one. Temper. Attitude. Maybe a hint of crazy thrown in. It was best he helped her on her way quickly as possible.

After her call she walked over toward him, eyes directed toward the ground. Gone was the swearing and abrupt behavior, replaced by a gentle tone and normalcy. "Um ... they put me through to Dennis. He's on a job at the moment and won't be able to get here for at least three hours." Her green eyes met his, making his breath hitch in his chest. "I don't really want to sit out here in the middle of nowhere in this heat for that long. Is there somewhere nearby where I can wait? Or I'm staying over at Harrigan's; it's not far from here. Is there any chance you could give me a lift? I'll call Dennis back to pick me up from there."

Troy nodded. Psycho-lady had gone, replaced by a smooth-talking, sweet and alluring woman who would have any man do as she commanded. Of course he'd help her; he was a gentleman after all. "Sure. I can do that."

She closed her eyes and took a calming breath. When she looked at him again, the tension fell away from her face and was replaced by the biggest, warmest of smiles. "Thanks, that would be great."

He couldn't deny this was one of the most attractive women he'd seen in a long time. Her smile held him captive and a long-distant memory of the same sensation flared up in his mind. He hadn't had a reaction like this since he met Nicola. Bah! What nonsense. Now if he could get his knee to stop tingling and itching like he had some contagious rash, all would be fine. He flicked at a fly that buzzed around his face, thankful for the distraction.

"I'm Kelleigh, by the way. I'll just grab my bags, if that's okay." She thumbed toward the trunk of her car.

"Troy," he said tipping his chin toward her. Still bamboozled by his reaction.

She eyed him suspiciously and notably kept her distance. He could understand her concerns at having to put faith in a total stranger. He wondered if there was anything he could do to put Kelleigh's mind at ease and let her know she was in safe hands. "Why don't you call Grace at Harrigan's, she's the manager, and tell her you're on your way."

She nodded and turned away from him to make the call. He was unable to take his eyes off her. He shouldn't stare. He shouldn't ogle. He shouldn't be admiring the view.

Once she'd spoken to Grace, Troy snapped out of it, helped put Kelleigh's luggage into the tray of his Landcruiser and headed toward Harrigan's. He grinned as she fanned herself in front of the air-conditioning vents.

"So what were you doing out here?" Troy asked as he turned on to Broke Road.

"I had a meeting at Larry Peterson's."

He glanced at her sideways but she remained focused on the road. With Larry's ill health of late, Troy wondered if his old neighbor was getting all his affairs into order.

"You're obviously not from around here. Are you a lawyer or something, from Sydney?"

"No, I'm not a lawyer." Her tone was edged with a touch of defensiveness. "Larry's a client and I'll be here in the Hunter for a few weeks of work. I drove up yesterday from Melbourne. I wanted to have my own transport while I'm here so I could get around and see the sights, but that obviously hasn't worked out in my favor."

"Dennis will look after you, but going by the damage done to your car, I would prepare yourself for the worst. I think it will be out of action for a while." There may be some small possibility Dennis could perform a miracle, but he doubted it.

Troy glanced in the mirror and winced. Damn it, he'd left his hat on. How rude of him. He quickly took it off and placed it on the seat beside him. He grinned, sensing her eyes upon him as he ruffled his hand through his short blond hair.

"Has anyone ever told you, you have the most beautiful eyes?" Shock flickered across her face as the words came unbidden. "I mean that as a compliment, not a pick-up line." She shrunk down in her seat and wiped her hands on top of her thighs. He caught a glimpse of her saying, "shit," under her breath as she turned away.

He resisted the temptation to laugh, but heat rose up the side of his neck and took up residence in his cheeks. "Thank you. I may have heard that once or twice before."

He focused on the road ahead as awkward silence filled the cabin, the sound of the rough engine offering some reprieve. Then her phone rang. She dived into her handbag, drew it out and looked at the caller ID. She gritted her teeth. "I don't want to talk to you now." She mumbled through her clenched jaw, jabbing her finger madly against the screen, trying to turn it off.

Troy's eyes widened as she stamped her feet on the floor and stuffed the phone back in her bag. She took a heaving breath, leaned back in the seat and wiped her hair back away from her face. "Sorry about that. I'm not in the mood to talk to lawyers about my ex-boyfriend at the moment."

"Nice chap, was he?" He grimaced at seeing the hurt glass over her eyes.

"I hope he rots in hell."

Troy parked his car outside the accommodation entrance at Harrigan's Irish Pub and Hotel and helped Kelleigh with her luggage into the reception area. As he placed the suitcase down on the ground in front of the counter, its heavy weight caused it to tip off balance and topple forward onto the tiles with a loud thud. He bent down to right the bag at the same time Kelleigh did. Their heads collided with a hard bump. He stood up quickly and reached out to steady Kelleigh from the blow. Goose bumps shot across his skin. When he looked up, her green eyes connected with his and he lost the ability to breathe.

Like earlier, the distant recall of reacting this way when he met Nicola twenty years ago set alarm bells off in his head. He should be hightailing it out of there as quick as his feet could carry him. But he was unable to move as he absorbed her stunning features. Dimples highlighted her left cheek when she smiled, long lashes outlined her flawless skin and her pink lips looked inviting and kissable. But beautiful or not, he'd done his Good Samaritan job for the day; it was time to get going.

"Are you okay?" he mumbled, clearing his throat.

"Yeah," she said as she rubbed her head. "Thank you so much for the ride. It's really appreciated."

"You're welcome. Dennis will look after you. Do you need anything else? Otherwise I'll be off." Yes, there were fences to be fixed. Grape crushers to mend. Trampled vines to salvage. Time to refocus on all that had to be done at Gumtrees.

"No. Thank you. I'll be fine."

With that, he took his cue to exit and headed out the door.

As he hopped in his Landcruiser, he glanced back into the reception area and saw Kelleigh booking into her room. He turned the key, started the engine and put the vehicle into gear. So much had happened since he'd started working back here in the Valley. Finding Jessica after all these years. Meeting his grown son, Conner. And now, a fleeting moment in time helping Kelleigh had stirred up long-forgotten feelings. Feelings he never thought he'd ever experience again. Feelings he needed to ignore; he had too much going on in his life. Harvest season, spending time with Conner and the expansion at Gumtrees needed all of his undivided attention.

He rubbed at his chest. His knee ached. What had Kelleigh done to him? No ... he needed to find Jett to fix the broken fence and then get back out in to the vineyard as soon as possible. A few hours of sweating it out while hard at work, before the sun set, would surely see an end to this craziness.

Chapter 3

Kelleigh looked up from signing the check-in paperwork and saw Troy drive out of the car park. He'd been so nice to offer her help while all she'd done was act like a raving lunatic. Yep, she'd made a downright fool of herself. But her pent-up anger, her helplessness and her fright at being stuck out in the middle of nowhere made her act all crazy. Stupid busted tire.

She'd never had to change a car tire in her life before. She was a construction engineer and on-site project leader who in the past had changed boring rods on auger drills without blinking an eye, but changing a tire had rendered her useless. Being stranded out in the middle of the countryside had her nerves on edge. She was petrified of being mugged or raped and left to die out on the side of the road, never to be found.

As Troy's car disappeared off into the distance, she sighed. After everything that had happened to her over the past few weeks, her car being wrecked was the last thing she needed. It was not normal for her to lose her temper, but a woman could only take so much crap before having to let off some steam. Troy must think she was an absolute nutcase. Oh well. It was a good thing he was gone.

But the vision of Troy's muscles flexing in the hot sun, and sweat making his shirt cling to his muscular back as he tended to her car flashed through her mind. Heat flushed her cheeks. Despite her outburst, she hadn't been oblivious to his fine physique and certainly didn't mind been rescued by someone so handsome. A sheepish smile touched her lips; she'd have to call Fran and tell her all about being rescued by one hunky farmer ... worker ... whatever or whoever he was. And he had the most amazing blue eyes she'd ever seen. She wanted to slap herself in the forehead when she'd verbalized her thoughts in front of him.

As she grabbed her luggage and walked past the glass doorway, she paused and looked out over the countryside, where farmland and lush vineyards stretched out over the rolling hills in all directions. The occasional house, cluster of sheds and dams dotted the landscape amongst the endless expanse of green. This area of Pokolbin in the Hunter Valley was breathtaking, and it was going to be a fabulous location for the new Japanese Lifestyle Golf Resort.

The tasks before her as the engineering project leader assigned to head up and supervise several feasibility studies were going to be a challenge. JLR had been in confidential acquisition discussions with Larry Peterson for a few months now, and she'd been at his place this morning discussing the schedule of work she and her team coming up from Melbourne would be carrying out over the next few weeks. Drilling for soil tests, gathering water samples and extensive surveying of every inch of the land would be time consuming and damn hot work in the middle of summer.

She let out an audible groan. Her boss, Toru, the project director, was coming up from Melbourne to the Hunter Valley a couple of times over the next few weeks to coordinate some of the other required studies. Unfortunately it was necessary, considering the time constraints. They had to ensure all the data for the feasibility assessment was collected in time to present their case for rezoning the land at the Cessnock City Council in four weeks.

Kelleigh had seen the preliminary designs for the resort from the golf course architects; the clubhouse and hotel were going to be five-star luxury. Toru and the lawyers must have done a fine job to convince the owner to sell. From colleagues at work she'd heard Toru was ruthless in negotiations. Everyone ended up saying yes to him. She'd only been working for JLR for three months and was yet to witness him in action.

But something about the man made her skin crawl. She wasn't able to put her finger on it. Maybe it was because of everything that had happened to her recently made her skeptical of everyone.

While she'd done work on many development projects over the years, this was her first time as a project leader. This was a huge construction project compared to what she'd done previously. Shop renovations, school buildings and small offices had been the extent of her prior experience.

She would've never have contemplated applying for a job like this, but Rodrigo had insisted. It was all about the money for him, rather than what she really wanted to do. Then again, she didn't know what that was either. For too long she'd let Rodrigo influence her decisions, and even let him submit her job application to JLR. She'd been surprised at landing an interview, shocked at being offered the role. So here she was in the middle of nowhere, out of her comfort zone but determined to give it her best shot.

She glanced at her watch. She had two hours until Dennis was due to pick her up to retrieve her coupe from the ditch, so she decided to settle into her room and have lunch. Dragging her suitcase behind her, she headed down the hallway and found her room. The one-bedroom suite was more than adequate for her stay. Kitchenette, lounge room with a decent-sized working desk. The fireplace looked like it got a workout during the cold winter months, but she'd be long gone by then. She dumped her bag in the main bedroom, flicked open the curtains and couldn't wait to laze about in the glorious king-sized bed and look out over the countryside through full-length glass windows and sliding doors.

She fell back onto the mattress feeling exhausted. With her arm bent, covering her eyes, she prayed this horrid day would come to an end. Tension mounted in her temples; she could feel the early stages of a headache starting to form. But her belly protested. It grumbled loudly and demanded food. Who was she kidding? There was no time to relax, so she hauled herself off the bed, changed into jeans and t-shirt, grabbed her handbag and headed back out the door and into the pub to grab lunch.

The cool air-conditioning brushed across her skin and felt like heaven as she entered the main area. She took a deep breath, drawing in the stale smell of beer that filled the air. The large glass doors closed with a gush of air behind her as she walked toward the bar. She eyed the green walls, the wood paneling of the bar, the rustic timber stools. A smile tugged at the corners of her mouth. An Irish pub in the middle of one of Australia's prime wine regions amused her. But she was from Melbourne, where just about every culture existed in some form or another within its vibrant streets. It was a welcome change to be away from all the quirky, excessively LED-lit, trendy venues she had visited on a regular basis. Yet another of Rodrigo's lifestyle choices. Here, there were no neon lights, designer lounges or flashy furniture. Just the old bar with a line of ales on tap and timber shelves covered with a diverse range of whiskies, scotches and liqueurs.

There were a few patrons sitting at the scattered wooden tables. Kelleigh perched herself up on one of the stools at the bar and started to peruse the menu as a short, plump, gray-haired woman with a welcoming smile made her way over toward her.

"Welcome to Harrigan's. Lovey, you look like you could do with a drink. Had a rough day, have you? What can I get you?"

Kelleigh glanced behind her at the bar fridge filled with bottled beer and other refreshments. It dawned on her that she hadn't ordered her own drinks for years. Rodrigo had always done it for her. She couldn't believe how many of the little things she had to take responsibility for herself once again. Did she have the strength to get through all this mess? "What do you recommend?" See, she still couldn't make a decision for herself.

"Oh lovey, you look like you could do with something with a bit of substance." The woman glanced up and down her slender frame. "You've come to an Irish pub, why don't you be a little adventurous? Why not try one of our beers on tap, a local wine or a good ol' Irish whisky? How about something to really satisfy your taste buds? How about a Kilkenny?"

Kelleigh hesitated a moment, ran her eye over the beer taps in front of her, her taste buds jumping with anticipation. "That sounds great. And are there any specials on the menu today?" she said, rescanning the bar menu before her.

"We have a delicious beef and Guinness pie; can I get you one of those?"

A pie? She hadn't had a meat pie of any kind in years; the thought of one now made her mouth water. Rodrigo had made her feel guilty if she indulged in food; overly worried she'd get fat. What a jerk he was. Why did she not realize what a control freak he'd been sooner, before she lost everything? The delicious smells from the kitchen drew her back to the menu. The pie sounded so good. "Yes please."

The bar attendant nodded, took a fresh glass and proceeded to pull the drink from the tap. "Thatta girl. So what brings you to this part of the world?"

"Work. I'm staying here in one of the hotel rooms for about a month."

"Ah-ha. Kelleigh, right? You called just before letting us know you were on your way. Glad to see you made it safely. I'm Grace. It's nice to meet you." Grace thrust her hand over the bar to shake.

"Likewise." Kelleigh shook hands before digging in her bag for her company credit card to pay for her order. At least this one would work.

"If you don't mind me saying, you look a little flustered. You okay?" Grace asked.

Kelleigh's shoulder slouched. "It's been one of those days. My car burst a tire, and as a result I've also managed to successfully damage just about every piece of mechanism underneath it as I careered off the road over near Larry Peterson's farm. A nice gentleman, Troy, gave me a lift here to get me out of the hot sun while I wait for the tow truck."

The women's eyes suddenly sparkled. "Oh. That would be Troy Smith who helped you. Right? He's not too shabby to look at, is he? Hasn't he got the most wickedly gorgeous eyes?" Kelleigh giggled while Grace cleaned the counter. "I shouldn't say things like that. I went to school with his mother and used to babysit him when he was a boy. He's grown into such a handsome man. After all the bad luck he's had with women, it's a shame he hasn't managed to find someone new to stick around."

Kelleigh huffed. Yeah, finding someone who committed to a relationship would be nice.

She wrapped her fingers around her glass and took a mouthful of the creamy amber liquid. She reached for a napkin and wiped away the froth that tickled her top lip. "I'm grateful he came along when he did, otherwise I would be out there for hours waiting for Dennis, the tow truck guy."

"No worries, love. You enjoy that drink. Your pie won't be long. I better go and attend to the other patrons who are all starting to glare at me. This mob knows I love 'em dearly, but they'll get their damn drinks when I'm good and ready." She pointed and winked at one of the men sitting at the opposite end of the bar, waiting patiently for his refill.

"Thank you," Kelleigh said. She wiped the condensation of her glass with the edge of her finger and watched Grace toddle off to serve the other waiting guests.

Kelleigh took another gulp of her drink and savored the bitter taste that lingered in her throat. She really liked the beer. It was the tiniest of steps toward finding herself again. Yes, she had a truckload of problems to deal with. A debt of $250,000 wasn't going to disappear overnight. But Rodrigo had. There'd be no more failed business ventures. No more gambling. No more stealing her money. No more fraudulent signatures to run up yet another credit card. Gone was the high-rolling lifestyle, along with the fancy fashion and expensive tastes. She'd never been one to be excited by all the glitz and glamor like Rodrigo had. The day her credit cards stopped working had been a blessing in disguise. As she stared at the amber liquid in the glass before her, she noted for the first time in weeks that the heaviness in her chest had eased.

This work trip, taking her miles away from her troubles, was the break she needed. Away from lawyers. Away from police investigations. Away from her life packed up in her sister's garage. Some distance away from everything was necessary so she could find herself again. Find her strength, her inner fight and renew her confidence. She needed to get her life back on track. She closed her eyes and wondered. Was that possible to do in just a few short weeks?

Chapter 4

Harrigan's pub was quiet for a Tuesday night; the bistro area was usually filled with families having early dinners. But tonight the patrons were scarce. A good chance to finish off some work without any interruptions.

After a hearty meal and catchup with Grace, Troy sat at a table in the corner going over the expansion plans for Gumtrees Winery. Design diagrams and notes covered the table before him. Coming into harvest season, every daylight hour was spent in the paddocks; nighttime was left for business administration. It still boggled his mind that he was now a joint owner with Nick and Maria. Six months on and plans were about to be executed to expand. He rubbed his eyes, tired from sitting and staring at his laptop screen for too long. He'd gone over the figures many times but he wanted one last check before he met with Nick to start the implementation steps. Their bottom line was healthy, but he wouldn't shy away from a few new supply contracts into another restaurant chain or two. The up and coming Hunter Valley Wine Trade Festival would hopefully present new opportunities.

He reached for his notepad and glanced down the column of figures. What he saw really excited him. Alongside the new function room and cabins they'd planned on building, he'd finalized all the necessary calculations for putting another few acres under trellis. He was meticulous with the detail and his months of hard work looked like it would come to fruition. This would increase their production significantly and boost their bottom line.

Troy scratched at his unshaven chin and considered the workload. They'd have to hire one or two more full-time staff. He chuckled to himself. The path in life that led him here had certainly been a rocky one, but he'd never felt so content and grounded in all his life. He had his son, Conner, and Gumtrees. Life couldn't get much better.

He grabbed his beer and drank the last of its contents before signaling to Grace behind the bar for another.

"You're working too hard," she said, placing a fresh glass on the table next to his paperwork and cleared away the empty one, along with his dinner plate.

"I'm fine." He stretched his neck from side to side and kneaded away a knot that had lodged itself in his shoulder. He glanced at the clock on the far wall of the pub. It showed it was a smidge past eight o'clock. He had a busy day tomorrow spraying the vines for bugs, so he'd better pull his finger out and finish entering this data into his laptop. He didn't have much more to do.

"Okay. You let me know if you need anything else." Grace turned on her heels and headed back behind the bar. For a fleeting moment he remembered growing up in nearby Cessnock; Grace had always been like a second mother to him. Many fun-filled hours were spent at her house, playing on her trampoline in the backyard and climbing the big old tree in the corner of her yard. All so long ago.

He turned his attention back to his notes and typed figures into his spreadsheet. When a shadow hindered the view of his papers he frowned and had to move them around to try and catch the light.

He was about to tell the person in his way to move. But when he looked up his eyes widened and pulse went up a notch. "Kelleigh. Hi."

"I didn't mean to disturb you. I wanted to say thank you again for all your help yesterday. Dennis came and picked me up and now my car is at his workshop. He's going to call me in a few days with an assessment of the damage and cost to fix it. The insurance assessor is apparently away on holidays. Lucky for me, work allowed me to hire a much-needed more practical four-wheel drive to get around the place without any more grief."

"I'm glad you're okay."

"Thanks."

An awkward silence hung in the air as Troy watched her tuck her hands into the rear pockets of her jeans and rock back on her heels. He tried to ignore the strange pull he had toward her. The flutter in the pit of his stomach should be the warning sign he needed to stay away. But for some reason he chose to ignore it and his palms started to sweat. Should he ask her to stay for a drink? No, she wouldn't want to do that.

His gaze drifted down, over her low-cut t-shirt stretched firmly across the curve of her breast and stopped at her midriff. The way her t-shirt grazed the top of her jeans and showed off her tanned skin when she moved was really sexy. Damn it. He hoped she didn't notice him checking her out.

"Okay then. Might catch you round," she said, starting to turn away.

"Would you like to join me for a drink?" The words had left

his mouth before he had time to think any further.

Her raven-black hair fanned out around her shoulders as she turned back to face him. He momentarily froze, in awe of her beauty.

"Are you sure? You look busy."

"I was just finishing up." He waved to the chair across from him and she nodded in acceptance. He stood up and rushed around to pull the chair out for her.

"What will it be?"

"Please, let me get the drinks. It's the least I can do to say thank you for your help."

While he appreciated the offer, he insisted on buying.

"All right, I'll have a Kilkenny."

"Excellent. I'll be back in a moment." Troy walked over to the bar and ordered the drinks from Grace, who gave him a cheeky wink when he picked up the beers and turned to head back to the table.

Kelleigh must have sensed him approach because she turned around and her green eyes locked on to his. He almost stumbled in his stride before he placed the drinks on the table and returned to his seat. What was with him tonight?

"What were you working on?" She eyed the notepad and laptop he had left open on top of the table. He saved his work, shut the laptop down, stuffed everything into his laptop bag and put it out of the way.

"I was just going over some business expansion plans. Costings, expenses, forecasts."

"What ... new grand schemes to make you millions of dollars?" she said with an air of disdain.

He was taken back by the negative vibe that suddenly radiated from her. Gumtrees' bottom line was healthy and their steady growth was sustainable for the coming years. He shrugged her doubts away. "It's necessary to keep up in a competitive market. We're not doing anything outrageous or out of our means." Nick and he didn't have grandiose plans like some of the other local vineyards that had become elaborate operations. That's why he loved Gumtrees, its boutique nature suited him perfectly.

"What is it that you actually do?" she asked.

"I'm a viticulturist."

"You work with grapevines all day. Fair enough," she said and took a swig of her beer. "So why are you here at the pub? Are you trying to avoid someone at home? Your wife? Girlfriend? Lover?"

He grinned and rubbed the back of his neck with his hand. "Actually, I have none of the above."

She raised her eyebrow in interest. "Really? How come a handsome guy like you is single?" He smiled over the rim of his glass, chuffed she thought he was handsome. "What's your story? Have you had a bad breakup, your partner died, you're still waiting to find that special someone?"

He coughed, nearly choking on his beer. What was meant to be lighthearted conversation unfortunately was his reality. "Well ... you got two out of three. Yes, I've had my share of breakups in the past and yes, my wife did die in a car accident."

"Holy shit!" Kelleigh gasped and covered her hand with her mouth. "I'm so sorry. I didn't mean—"

"It's okay. It happened a long time ago. Nine years to be exact." His guts knotted, remembering that day as if it was yesterday. The phone call from the police. The rush to the hospital. Having to identify his Nicola's bloodied body.

He remembered fighting with her that morning. As usual, it was more from his frustration at feeling so helpless, not knowing how to help her break out of her depression. It had been another day where she had refused to get out of bed. Yet another day where she got lost in the deep dark places in her mind.

No matter how much he assured Nicola he loved her with all his heart and he would stand by her until the end of time, some days it was never enough. When the call came from the police, guilt consumed him for so long. He blamed himself, he believed it had been their argument that sent her off that bridge.

The police found no evidence of another vehicle causing the accident. There was nothing wrong with the car. Her autopsy found her system loaded with medication. Troy was convinced she committed suicide. Was it her way of freeing everyone infected by her illness? It freed her parents. It freed him. It had freed her from her darkness. Is that a selfish way of looking at it now? He'd done everything possible to help her— the counseling, the support groups, the therapy. Nothing was ever enough.

Closing his eyes he could still picture her beautiful face, her dark green eyes and her smile. The good times did outweigh the bad. But sometimes it was hard not to see the scars on her wrists from self-harming. Her horrific nightmares. The secrets that took years for her to reveal. The depression finally pulled her under.

Time had healed a lot of the pain but not erased the memory. In the years that followed he tried to move on. Meet other women. He'd had a glimmer of hope with Jessica, but who was he kidding. His heart died that day with Nicola. But he'd found happiness and fulfillment in other things—his work, his involvement in the community and building on his relationship with his son.

"So, what?" Kelleigh's hand touched her throat. "You haven't been with anyone in nine years?"

That made him laugh and he waved over at Grace behind the bar for another round of drinks. "No, I'm not saying that at all."

Grace placed the fresh ales down on the table and quickly departed with the empties.

Kelleigh relaxed her shoulders, looking relieved he wasn't some clogged-up, celibate mourner. Life had dealt him several rough blows and somehow he'd made it through them all.

She took a big drink, leaving a line of foam behind on her mouth. He sat there mesmerized as he watched her lick her lips slowly with her tongue. *Lucky lips!* He struggled to collect his thoughts and had to change the subject. "Why were you at Larry's this morning?"

She shook her head. "I'm really sorry, but I can't say anything because there is a confidentiality agreement in place."

"You can't even tell me what you do?"

"Nope." She slouched, looking exasperated. "Look, I don't want to talk about work, ex-boyfriends, politics or religion. I don't want to have to think about anything for a while."

Kelleigh drew the glass to her lips and proceeded to scull the contents. Troy was more than happy to not delve further into his past or talk about work. So the mystery surrounding her still remained as the conversation skirted around simple things like travel and nothing in particular. But if she was staying here in the Hunter for a few weeks, someone would talk soon enough. Things never stayed a secret for long in this community.

She turned around in her seat, waved at Grace with two fingers to order another round of drinks. Troy hesitated. He'd had a few drinks already so one more and he wouldn't be able to drive home. Oh well, it would be another night sleeping on the couch at Grace's. She was still babysitting him even after all these years.

Grace delivered two more drinks and winked once more at him as she turned to leave. Good 'ol Grace. Always keeping an eye on everyone and everything. But she had nothing to worry about; this was just an innocent drink. Or two. No wait, he was up to number three. Even four. He turned his attention to Kelleigh and was surprised to see her downing mouthfuls of her beer again. "Hey, I forgot to ask. How's your foot after kicking your tire yesterday?"

She snorted when she laughed and covered her mouth with her hand.

"Oh no. Did I just snort?"

That only made her laugh more; the contagious sound got to him and he joined in. She picked up her napkin and wiped tears from her eyes. She was beautiful when she smiled. "I'm sorry for my behavior yesterday. I've had one drama after the other lately. I'm normally not like that."

He leaned forward to rest his arms on the table. "I'm glad to hear that. I must admit I was concerned for my own safety. You looked like you were going to throw that wrench my way at any moment."

She giggled. "Me? I wouldn't hurt a fly."

"I was keeping my distance. Then you started kicking the tire, I thought you were going to break your foot."

She lowered her eyes, her long lashes brushed against her skin. "I have to admit it's still sore."

"I've been known to give a pretty good foot massage." Troy gulped hard after the words had left his mouth. He tugged at his shirt collar as heat rose up his neck at making such a suggestive comment.

But Kelleigh placed her beer down and leaned forward onto the table as well. Her green eyes narrowed to provocative slits. "If you're not careful, I might take you up on your offer. I do love a good foot massage."

Troy's heart missed a beat and his groin stirred. Kelleigh was making all parts of his body rise to attention. It was ridiculous, but hey, he was a guy, and surely no harm could come from a bit of flirting. "My foot massages are good, but nothing beats my shoulder massage."

"I don't know about that. I mean, look at those rough hands of yours." She reached across the table, took his hand in hers and turned his palm upward. "They look like they've seen some tough times. They're all scratched and callused. You're trying to tell me you give a great massage?"

He tried to keep his breath at a normal pace, but Kelleigh was causing heat to surge through his veins. He hadn't had sex in months and now, after a few drinks … well … his intent for an innocent drink was being corrupted. Was he reading her playful comments and body language correctly? It would be nice to let off some steam and have a night between the sheets. She wasn't in town for long and that was a good thing that led to no complications.

"Only you can be the judge of that. I'm willing to be put to the test." Apprehension tugged at his chest as he waited for her response. He sat still, unable to move. Shivers crossed his skin as Kelleigh continued to play with his hand. Her fingers rubbing against his palm sent a jolt coursing through his body and he could feel his erection starting to rise to the occasion. He had to do something fast. Either take her back to her room or leave to crash on Grace's couch.

Kelleigh stopped and looked him straight in the eye. Had he been too forward? Damn it, he was so out of practice meeting women. But then she edged closer toward him across the table.

"I know you don't know me at all; but believe me, after everything that's been going on in my life it'd be nice to let my hair down for a while, figuratively speaking, and to have some fun. So … I'm keen. Are you?"

His whole body stood to attention as she withdrew her hold of his hand, grabbed her glass and consumed the rest of her beer.

Troy didn't waste a moment. "I'll get the bill."

He grabbed his laptop bag, stood up and helped Kelleigh from her chair. He quickly spoke to Grace who was clearing the table next to them, no doubt eavesdropping in on their conversation. "Can you add all the drinks and stuff to my account, please? I'm, er ..." Feeling lost for words and with other things now on his mind, he didn't utter another word as he turned and followed Kelleigh out the door.

Chapter 5

Kelleigh swayed as she walked toward the door of her room. She'd had four schooners of beer and was feeling buzzed from the effects of the alcohol. Troy's enchanting eyes had held her captivated during drinks, even though his attempts at flirting were poor. But hey, she wouldn't have done any better. She was happy he was talking to her and not running off screaming in the other direction, thinking she was a raving lunatic after her episode yesterday.

She glanced over her shoulder and caught sight of his smoldering sapphire gaze. The way he looked at her made butterflies take flight in her stomach. She tried to recall if this was how Jamie looked at Fran? In reality it was probably the alcohol making her feel this way, but it was nice to think otherwise for a moment.

She paused at her door and admired Troy's blond hair, sun-kissed skin and naturally well-muscled physique. Completely opposite to Rodrigo's dark complexion, protein-powder induced muscles and moisturized baby-soft skin. Completely different to Rodrigo's not-a-hair-out-of-place appearance. She lowered her eyes; her confidence wavered. Could she do this? Should she be doing this a month after Rodrigo had left? Why not? This was one night. She needed this. Something reckless. Something fun. Something to make her feel like a woman again. One small step toward gaining control back of her life.

Kelleigh's hands trembled as she opened her handbag and rummaged around for her room key. The anticipation of having those hands of Troy's on her body was enough to make her break out in a feverish sweat. This had to be the most reckless thing she'd ever done in her life. She'd always been one to approach relationships carefully. Go on dates before sleeping with someone. Get to know them. Meet their parents. Bah! Look where that had left her.

Finally locating her key, she tried to insert it into the lock. Unable to focus clearly, her hand swayed over the slot, from side to side. She inhaled sharply as Troy's warm breath on her neck shot goose bumps down her spine. He slowly reached around her and placed his hand on hers to steady it. With a gentle lean in toward her, he inserted the key and twisted the handle to open the door. The feel of his body against her hip sent her pulse racing and fire curling through her veins. "Smarty-pants," she said as she walked inside, flicked on the entryway light and made her way into the living area to shut the curtains.

Troy closed the door behind him, placed his bag on the ground and walked over to stand behind her. Shivers danced across her skin as he moved her hair away from her neck and planted a kiss beneath her lobe.

"Do you want a drink or something from the minibar?" she asked, savoring the sensation of his lips on her skin.

He shook his head as he stepped closer, weaved his arms around her waist and spun her around to face him. His sapphire eyes burned with desire as he drew her hard up against his body and planted his lips on hers.

No talking. No chitchat. This was perfect. Just sex. This was what she needed. She gasped for breath as her tongue danced with his. Running her hands up over his arms, the feel of his strong muscles beneath the cotton fabric of his shirt made her head dizzy. Finally she had her hands on him, and she did love a good pair of well-toned arms.

Troy paused and sucked air deep into his lungs, his hands resting on the small of her back. She didn't want him to stop, because if she thought about this too much longer, sense may take over. And at this point in time she wanted none of that. She wanted him. Weaving her fingers into his short blond hair, she drew him back to her, tasting his lips again. Luckily he obliged. Warm air enveloped around her and filled her senses with the alluring scent of his spicy aftershave.

His hardened groin pressed against her as he tightened his hold. As his hands explored the curve of her buttocks, the length of her thigh and up over her side toward her breast, the want escalated inside her. His tender touch, the deep rumble in his throat and his kisses made her feel … sexy. It had never been like this with Rodrigo.

Troy slid his arms around her stomach and turned her around to stand with her back against his chest. She caught sight of their reflection in the mirror as he nibbled on her ear and trailed kisses down the side of her neck. Her eyelids fluttered closed when his hands crept up over her shirt and cupped her breasts. Arching into his touch, her nipples hardened against his playful taunts.

"You're so beautiful," he whispered into her ear.

He nudged his groin into her so she could feel the hardness of his erection. "Open your eyes. I want you to see how sexy you are."

Hesitant at first, she refocused on the mirror. Under the soft lights reflecting golden off his skin, standing there wrapped in his arms, she felt safe and secure. All her inhibitions fell away.

Troy's fingers fumbled for the bottom of her t-shirt and hoisted it up over her head and tossed it aside onto the floor before returning to torment her aching nipples. His soft, gentle kneading through the fabric of her bra made her body temperature rise up another notch.

She giggled as her stomach muscles flinched when his hands slid down to the top of her waist, popped open the top button of her jeans and inched the zipper down. Slowly. Gradually. Controlled. His teasing fingers brushing over her cotton panties made every one of her nerve endings stand on end. Circling around in tiny playful movements he tickled her, sought out the edge of the elastic and slipped his fingers underneath. Gentle swirling strokes meandered lower and lower, making their way down to her opening. He slid his firm finger in between the folds of her skin; her whole body quivered as he met her arousal. A guttural groan resonated in her ear while his hot kisses lingered on her fiery skin.

"You feel so good," he said, stroking through her wetness and tantalizing her sweet spot.

Her legs wanted to curl beneath her but he held her tightly wrapped within his arms. The reflection of him touching her was intimidating at first, but now she didn't care. A smile tugged at the corner of his lips as he cupped her breast with one hand while the other lingered down her pants. As his fingers probed deeply in to her, his thumb rubbed relentlessly against her clitoris, her hips started pulsing gently in time with his masterful strokes.

Her breaths became more desperate as she reached up over her shoulder and touched the side of his face. She bit her lip, knowing she was close to coming. His fingers were doing wonders to her as her thighs strained to keep her upright.

As he tweaked her nipple, he applied just the right amount

of pressure to the swollen bud between her legs. She gasped as her orgasm ripped through her body. Her legs trembled like an earthquake measuring seven on the Richter scale, but Troy held her firmly against his chest.

"I do like seeing you orgasm," his breath hot on her neck while he watched her quaking body in the mirror. She turned her head away, embarrassed. "Don't look away. You're so beautiful. Can't you see that?"

"I'm looking at you, not myself," she said, drawing his attention to other things. Removing his hands from her pants, she turned toward him, placed her hands on his chest and felt his heart race beneath her touch. The sizzle beneath her fingertips had her anxious to feel his skin. His eyes never left hers as she undid the buttons of his shirt, peeled it from his shoulders and started to fold it neatly.

"What are you doing?" Troy asked, his brow furrowed.

"I'm putting your shirt—" She gasped when Troy reefed it out of her hands and threw it on the floor.

"I want to have sex with you. Not fold laundry."

She was in love with Troy already. Not literally, of course. But he won her over then and there. Rodrigo had always ensured that his designer threads were folded and carefully hung away in the closet before anything went on in the bedroom. Troy's disregard for his clothing was something she could get used to.

With hungry eyes, she surveyed the hard plane of his chest dusted with a splash of hair. Well-toned muscles rippled in the soft light as he moved. His solid waistline, smooth and firm, flinched as she clawed her nails over the surface of his skin. Hooking her fingers through his belt, she undid the buckle followed by the zipper on his jeans. Feeling his penis bulge beneath her fingertips sent pleasurable shockwaves coursing from her hand, up through her body and right down to her toes.

Boots and jeans were promptly removed before Troy's

hands laced around her once again. Her breath became more erratic as she took in every inch of his flesh. So much for those leathery, callused hands; she was amazed at how his touch was so soft.

He cupped her breast, leaned down and playfully nipped at it through the light padding of her bra. Her head fell back in bliss. With little effort, he unclasped her bra and let it fall away.

He groaned as he took one of her nipples into his mouth and sucked and licked her skin. If she wasn't careful she was going to come again; she grinned.

She weaved her hands through his hair, tugged on it slightly and drew his lips back to hers. Troy's hands drew around her, grabbed her ass and pulled himself against her. Carefully he guided her to take a few steps back into the bedroom until her knees butted up against the side of the bed.

Reaching down, she grabbed handfuls of the bedding and ripped the covers aside before returning to kiss the tip of his shoulder and trail her fingernails up his spine in featherlight strokes.

The look in his eyes made her breath catch in her throat. Such intensity. Such desire. Such want.

It was a split second that caught her by surprise. A flash of sadness flickered in his eyes, which made her heart lurch in her chest. Maybe this is what they both needed. A night to forget their problems, their past, their everything. Momentarily, anyway. Tomorrow the sun would rise and reality would have to be faced. Until then, she was going to have some fun.

Hunger returned to his eyes as he gently pushed her down onto the bed. He stood before her and rid himself of his trunks, freeing his hard erection. *Oh my Lord!* It was impressive, towering in the darkness before her. That thing could do some permanent damage. While grinning, he whisked off her panties and came forward to settle down on top of her. Skin against skin. Mouth against mouth. Body against body.

"Bugger! Stay there." He pulled away abruptly, jumped off the bed and dashed out of the room.

What the hell happened? Did she do something wrong? She propped herself up on her elbows, looked around helplessly and wondered what was going on. *Thank you*, she said to the heavens when he returned seconds later with his wallet and saw him remove a condom.

Lucky Troy had one of those, because she certainly didn't have any. Sex had not been on her agenda at all. What a letdown that would've been, to get this far and then, because of a lack of protection wouldn't be able to … Although … think about all the other activities they could have done that didn't involve penetration. *Hmmm.*

He waved the packet around playfully as he crawled back on to the bed.

"Allow me." She grabbed the condom and smiled mischievously before ripping it open and carefully rolling the rubber down over his steel-like shaft. Her eyes never left his while she listened to his jagged breath. Grazing her fingers through his soft pubic hair and rubbing her hand along his hardened rod, she ensured the condom was in place. So firm. So hard. So ready.

Troy's reassuring smile was all she needed as she lay back on the bed, drawing him to lie down on top of her. She wrapped her legs around his and melted into the mattress. His naked skin connecting with hers.

Gliding her fingers up along the full length of his arms, his hairs tickled her fingertips as they ran over the surface. Wriggling her hips, she drew her legs wider and felt the warm head of his erection press hard against her. He nudged at her opening. Teased her. Tormented her. Tantalized her with his rock-hard shaft. Delving into her arousal gently at first before sliding his full length deep into her. Her eyes widened in shock as her body adjusted to accommodate his size. Oh, yeah. So much bigger than Rodrigo.

As his hand shimmied over her flesh and curled around her thigh, he drove into her slowly, in and out, penetrating her deeper with every thrust. Her inner core clenched around him as he continued to plunge into her. Harder. Her breaths came shorter and sharper as she clawed into his back and tried to pull his body closer. Desperate for more connection. Meeting her demands and with a low rumbling in his throat, Troy buried himself within her.

She gasped when he hit a sensitive spot deep within her. His eyes glimmered with satisfaction as he repeated the same maneuver. The sound of her panting filled the air and her whole body tensed, begging for release. He tilted and jutted his hips against hers again and she was gone.

Digging her fingers into his back, every inch of her exploded as the toe-curling orgasm ripped through her. A guttural groan surged from Troy's throat as he came; his body quivered above her. Her heart pounded as the seismic pulse coursed through her system. It was as if every knot and bit of tension that had built up over the past month had finally left her body. She should have had sex with a stranger sooner. It certainly achieved her goal of wanting to forget the dramas of the past few weeks.

Savoring the feel of him inside her, the sensual kiss he gave her filled her with tender warmth, sending her heart aflutter. This was new. Maybe this was how great sex was supposed to make you feel. Maybe she'd just had an average sex life and this now raised her benchmark to a whole new level. Maybe size made a difference after all, but Troy's skill ... After a lingering kiss on her lips, he withdrew and fell beside her. With a goofy smile on her face, she cuddled into his arms. "I don't know about you, but that was just what I needed. Thank you."

Did you thank someone for sex? Was that what you said on a one-night stand?

"No complaints here," he said, his pulse still thundering through the veins visible in the side of his neck.

Kelleigh drew the cool cotton sheet over their bodies and curled in next to Troy. Every one of her limbs felt like jelly, all wobbly and useless. She was no expert at lovemaking; hell, she'd only been with a handful of guys in the course of her life to date, but something about Troy was different. The connection. The way he fit inside her. The way her body hummed when his lips were pressed against hers had her questioning her sanity. Troy felt so good and so right. What was with that? She'd only met him the previous day and this was not meant to be anything serious.

All this talk inside her head was silly nonsense and going nowhere fast. Troy was so not her type anyway. He sounded too much like Rodrigo with big plans, new projects and money-sucking ideas. Ha! She'd heard it all before and didn't want to be near anyone like that ever again. Troy would be out of her bed and gone soon enough.

He rested his cheek against her head as she circled her fingers across his chest. Her eyelids started growing heavy as she listened to the rhythmic beat of his heart and he combed his fingers through her hair. He didn't have to go just yet.

"Would you like to stay, or is there somewhere else you have to be?" Having him here beside her, holding him close for a while longer, would ward off reality for a little bit longer.

Silence filled the room as his chest rose and fell beneath the touch of her hand. Had she asked too much? A one-night stand was fine with her; she thought for one crazy moment it would be nice to wake up next to him. See those eyes in the morning light. Stupid, right?

"I can stay. That'd be nice because I'm not sure if my legs

would be able to carry me out of here at the moment." He kissed her hair and cuddled her.

She inhaled the scent of his spicy skin and nestled closer to him. This stranger in her bed for one night was just the therapy she needed.

Chapter 6

Troy snuck out of Kelleigh's room at six o'clock in the morning and successfully avoided running into Grace as he tiptoed down the hallway, out the door to his Landcruiser and headed back out to Gumtrees. What a night it had been. Unexpected. Spontaneous. Hot. He grinned as he rolled his shoulder and stretched out his arm, trying to work out the soreness and stiffness from where Kelleigh slept soundly on it during the course of the night. The ache was definitely worth it.

He'd barely slept a wink. The stirring in his stomach had not settled, along with his inability to think straight, an escalated heart rate and clouded vision. The only way to describe it was like an irreversible chemical reaction had gone off in his head. It had his mind racing; why did he have to have such an attraction to someone temporary? Kelleigh was a one-night fling. That's all there was to it, because he never wanted to risk another broken heart, disappoint anyone or lose somebody ever again. Life was good as it was.

Pulling into Gumtrees, he parked his Landcruiser in the shed and headed straight for the barn. He gathered two buckets of lucerne chaff and made his way over to the horse yards to feed Mustang and Sterling their breakfast before heading out into the vineyard. Glancing up, he saw Nick striding toward him. Troy tipped the buckets of food into the feed bins hanging on the rails and placed them on the ground as Nick neared him. Troy pushed the rim of his hat up to greet him. "Hey Nick. Morning."

"Crashed at Harrigan's again, did you?" Nick smirked, noticing he had the same attire on as last night. "You gotta stop crashing on the couch at Grace's. Can't be good for your health."

"No couch last night, mate." Troy lowered his eyes and couldn't wipe the grin off his face.

"Ah. A good night, hey?" Nick slapped him hard on his back and laughed heartily. "Good to see you're not hung up on Jessica anymore."

"You should know me better than that. I'm not hung up on her. Haven't been for ages."

Troy scratched at his unshaven chin. He couldn't deny he'd put in a decent amount of effort to rekindle his relationship with Jessica a couple of years ago, but he'd had to admit the spark wasn't there between them anymore. Twenty years had passed since high school and they'd both grown in different directions. She was all about big cities, the corporate life and the rich lifestyle to go along with it. To see her again after so many years, when he returned to the Hunter Valley, was both wonderful and shocking. To find out he'd left her pregnant the night he took off for America when he was seventeen, and she'd raised their son without him, shattered him to the core. With great effort, they'd managed to become friends again. He may not have won her heart, losing out to Nate Somers, hotel billionaire extraordinaire, but he'd gained a son. Conner turned twenty-two in a few months. Troy still found it hard some days to fathom, but he relished every moment he spent with him.

Jessica would always have a place in his heart, Nicola even more so. No other encounter proved to be more meaningful. But something about being with Kelleigh last night had him questioning his state of mind. He hadn't felt the need to have a partner in his life. Was that starting to change? But who'd want to be out here? Who'd want to live away from the big city lights in the country? Who'd want a man whose heart was incomplete? Oh no, was this his midlife crisis?

Visions of being with Kelleigh flickered through his mind. The very thought of her made his nether regions stir. She was feisty, mysterious and openly admitted to having a truckload of problems that were best left untouched. Still, it was hard not to think about her.

"On that note, you know Jessica's coming back in a couple of weeks to run the Wine Trade Festival and wants to stay here. Nate and the baby will be with her, that all right with you?"

"Nate? Sure, it's all fine by me." Troy no longer felt jealous twinges at the sound of the man's name who had won Jessica's heart. Nate was a good man and the perfect match for Jessica.

Usually Jessica called or emailed him, but he'd been occupied last night and hadn't been home to check for any messages this morning. Troy hadn't seen her in about six months; he couldn't keep track of her whereabouts, with her jet-setting lifestyle and living between England and Australia. Her business, Kick Event Management and Marketing, had expanded successfully overseas since she did the opening of the new Somers Hotel on Darling Harbour two years ago. Her job seemed like too much stress for his liking.

"I also got a call from a property developer. JRL or JLR ... something like that. They want a meeting with us next Tuesday to talk about a project they want to build in the region. It sounds like more of a nice meet and greet than anything else. I think you should be in on it. I'll email you the calendar invite."

"Okay, count me in." Troy said. There was so much property development going on throughout the Valley, it would be interesting to see what was in the pipeline.

"You fixed that crusher yet?"

"No. Haven't found the problem. I'm sure it's something really simple like a jam. I'll get to it before the week is out, but today I have to spray the top verdelho paddock, the lower chardonnays tomorrow, and then Conner's coming up for the weekend. He can help me fix Larry's fence since he's sick again and Jett's away. I only managed a makeshift repair job on Monday afternoon. Time has got away from me since then and I haven't managed to get back to fix it properly."

"Geez, Larry's not well, is he? I'll go over and visit him later on and see how he's doing." Nick rubbed his arm while worry etched his brow, and then changed to his favorite subject. "How's the fruiting? Later on, can you bring up a sample of the semillon for testing in the lab? We have to watch these babies to make sure the sugar levels are just right for picking. We should only be a few weeks off harvesting."

Troy grinned and kicked his boot into the dirt. It was a typical morning catch-up with Nick, running through everything going on around the vineyard. "I'll meet you in the lab about three-thirty after spraying today. If it doesn't rain too much, we'll be right in four to five weeks to harvest."

"Excellent. We also need to get together and discuss the final expansion plans and implementation strategies. Harvest will be over before we know it. I'll send you a message later on today with a suitable time to catch up. Might have to wait until early next week for that."

"Fine with me. I went through everything again last night. I'm really happy with it. Even have room to accommodate some new trellises."

"Sounds good. I gotta get going so I'll leave you to it. Have a good day, you sly 'ol dog. Good to see you getting some action at last. At least one of us is. Maria's always too tired these days." Nick chuckled as he turned around and headed back over to the office.

Troy watched Nick depart and caught sight of several couples on their holiday stay weave their way along the pathways from their cabins toward the restaurant to have breakfast. He caught the faint smell of bacon wafting in the breeze, which made his tummy grumble. He, too, had better grab some food before heading out to spray.

"Hey. What's that for?" Mustang, the old well-loved quarter horse popped his head over the railing and nudged him in the arm for his morning ear rub. He grinned as he scratched the horse behind the ears. Mustang pushed his neck harder against Troy's hand; closed his eyes and twitched his ears in delight. "You know I give good massages, don't you?"

Not too much of that went on last night when he was with Kelleigh, but he was sure he'd touched every inch of her skin. The majority of it with his mouth. He inhaled deeply, still smelling her scent upon his skin and clothing. It had been a great night, but the fun was over. He sighed as he picked up the grain bucket and headed back into the barn. Time to face the day. That spraying wouldn't get done on its own.

Chapter 7

Late on Friday afternoon, Troy stood on the veranda of his cottage and watched the trickle of weekend guests arriving. The icy-cold beer in his hand was quenching his thirst after a hot hard day's work out in the field. As he finished off the last mouthful, Conner's silver Audi made its way up the driveway and parked in front of his home.

Even though it had been two and a half years since finding out he had a grown son, some days laying eyes on Conner still felt like the very first time Jessica brought him out to Gumtrees. He'd never be able to make up for all the years he was absent, but swore to himself he wouldn't miss another day in his son's life. Progress was slow, but at least they had become friends.

Conner stepped out of the car and waved in his direction. Board shorts, surf shirt and flip-flops made Conner look like he was going to the seaside for the weekend, not to work in the vineyard. He grabbed his bag and a case of beer from the rear seat of the car before taking the steps up into the cottage.

"S'up," Conner said as he placed the beer onto the small kitchen table and dropped his bag onto the ground. Troy gave him a manly hug hello and patted him on the back.

"What have you been doing today? You stink like a chemical spill." Conner waved his hand in front of his screwed-up nose.

"Probably do. I've been spraying all day so I'd better go and take a shower. Wanna beer while I go and clean up? There's cold ones in the fridge."

"Hell yeah." Conner helped himself to the fridge and restocked it with the beer he'd bought.

After a refreshing cold shower to rid himself of the spray and dirt, Troy walked out of the bathroom to find Conner had well and truly made himself comfortable. There he was, lazing on the blue couch with his feet resting up on the coffee table, watching the start of the evening innings of the day/night cricket match.

"What's for dinner?" Conner asked as he stood up and grabbed himself and Troy another beer from the fridge.

"I thought you'd bring up something?"

"Nope. Totally forgot."

"Well then, it's leftovers. There's a casserole I made the other night I can reheat. The restaurant is booked out tonight, so we'll leave the kitchen staff in peace."

"Whatever. As long as I don't have to cook, it's fine with me."

Troy busied himself in the kitchen, surprised when Conner pitched in to help. He set the small table with plates and cutlery, even toasted and buttered some bread.

"No Becky with you this weekend?" Troy asked Conner about his long-term girlfriend. Troy's heart lurched in his chest when Conner squeezed his eyes shut tightly and looked away. "What's happened?"

"We broke up ... well ... actually ... she dumped me." Conner sculled his beer and grabbed another before flopping down on the chair at the table.

"What? Why?" he asked, placing a plate of hot food in front

of his son.

The shrug. The grunt. The uncomfortable shuffle. That damn flick of the long fringe that hung over his eyes. "It's been brewing for a long time. When I went and stayed with Mum in London for two months in June, that was the start of our problems. I mean, the sex was still great, but we'd grown apart. Still sucks though. We'd been together for four years."

"Sorry to hear that. She was a nice girl. Oh, well, there are plenty of young single ladies out there. You're a good-looking, decent young man; I don't think you'll have any issue of meeting someone new when the timing's right."

Conner rolled his eyes as he chewed on a mouthful of food. "What, you're now an expert on dating. When was the last time *you* went out with someone?"

Troy couldn't restrain the smile that crept across his face as he took a bite of his dinner.

"What's that? What's that goofy grin on your face?" Conner waved his fork in his direction. "There's something different about you. Oh no, did you inflict yourself on to some poor woman? That's so gross."

Troy tried not to choke on his mouthful of food at his son's observations. He felt his cheeks burning and he didn't think it was from the hot plate of dinner before him. Every time he was with Conner, somehow the kid managed to embarrass him.

"Okay. We're both adults so I won't deny it." Troy took a swig of his beer. "I had a pleasant evening with a lady I met the other night. Let's just say I still know how to ride the ol' horse, if you get my drift." He winked.

"Ew!" Conner turned up his nose. "But it's about time. You haven't been with anyone since Mum left."

"You know your mother and I never got back together, no matter how much I tried.'

"Yeah, but you were hung up on her for ages."

"Maybe. Maybe we're all only supposed to have that one great love in our life. If that's the case, I had Nicola."

"But she was a nut job."

A stab of pain struck the center of his chest. Ouch! "Come on now. Most of the times we had together were good. She was adventurous, fun-loving and had a great, quirky sense of humor. But, yes, once the bad days started, they gradually grew worse. It never changed how much I loved her."

"I'm sorry. I didn't mean to be rude."

"I know you didn't." It didn't help the ache in his heart subside quickly though. "Did you love Becky?"

"I guess I did, but it wasn't rock-your-world shit like you described with Nicola. We were just good mates."

"Well then, there's hope for you yet. Me ... I may have used up all my credit."

"So, what? You're not seeing the chick from the other night again?"

"Doubt it. She's only in town for a few weeks on a job before she heads back to Melbourne." He tried hard not to think about Kelleigh and the weird feeling inside him that hadn't subsided. Surely it would disappear soon. "Well, that's enough about our dismal love lives for now. Tomorrow I need to fix a fence, would you like to help me out?"

"Sure. Whatever. I'll do the dishes later, but right now can we watch the cricket?"

"Sure." With that, they both stood and headed for the couch.

***

"How's the job hunting going?" Troy asked Conner while unraveling the fencing wire off the roll.

"It sucks." Conner grunted as he threaded the length of barbed wire through the pole and attached the fence strainer to it. "I've been out of uni. for nearly twelve months and haven't found anything."

"What's next then? Are you going back to do more study? What about doing your Masters? Any ideas?" Troy asked while cutting the wire.

"I don't know. Working at Pepe's Pizza is okay for now, but it's not my choice of career. There's no jobs in architecture anywhere. Stupid degree. Should have studied something else. I've applied for jobs all over the country but nothing's come up."

"What about your mother? She got any contacts?"

Conner shook his head. "Nah. I'm going to help her out at the Wine Trade Festival in a couple of weeks. I don't mind doing the odd event with her to earn some money, but it's not my thing. She's offered me full-time work at Kick and even Nate said I could work at the hotel in Darling Harbour if I wanted to, but I haven't said anything either way. I'm not sure I want to be in hospitality either. I've hated having to move back home because I can't afford rent on my part-time wage. Guess I'm lucky Mum's hardly ever at home."

"Can I throw something into the mix for you to think about?" Troy inhaled deeply, humbled by the fact that he was in a position where he could help his son. "You've been so determined about finding work I didn't want to interfere, but why don't you consider coming to work out here? There's plenty of opportunity. There's everything from the viticulture side of things, to winemaking, to production and maintenance to working in the restaurant, sales or administration. Pay's nothing like the big city, but it's there for the taking."

"Really?" Conner stopped and looked up from attaching the next wire into place. The glimmer in his son's eyes made Troy's heart feel full within his chest. He'd do anything for Conner. Having him out here working by his side would mean so much.

Give him the chance to get to know him after so much time lost. "Can I think about it?" Conner looked lost in thought as he looked out across the vineyard before him.

"Sure. Harvest starts in a few weeks. Could use the extra hands if you're keen."

"I could be. I'll let you know." Conner adjusted his leather work-gloves on his hands before he strained the wire tight and wrapped the ends around the strand to secure it into place. "Let's get this damn fence finished."

Chapter 8

Kelleigh sipped on coffee in her room and went through the long list of emails early on Monday morning. Rolls of maps, printouts of project requirements and notes littered the desk. She'd spent all of last week at meetings in nearby Maitland and Cessnock and finalizing the requirements for her feasibility studies. All weekend she'd plotted out on her maps where to conduct the soil and water tests on Larry's place. With having to oversee the team out on-site as well as coordinate the other contractors, she didn't know where she was going to find the time to get everything done.

Her phone rang loudly. Sifting around under the pile of papers she finally found it. She didn't recognize the caller ID, but it appeared to be a local number. Maybe it was Troy from the other night? How would he know her number? She swiped the screen to answer, holding her breath waiting to hear the voice.

"Hello Miss Johnstone, it's Dennis."

She sighed with disappointment. "Hey Dennis. Thanks again for helping me last week. So what's the verdict on my car?" She braced herself for the damage bill.

"I'm sorry it took so long but the assessor has been away on holidays. But after his review on Friday, unfortunately I don't have any good news. After going over your car we've both agreed there is too much damage underneath it—to the fuel line, axle, chassis, etcetera—we've decided it would cost too much to fix. The car has to be written off."

"What? Written off? But ... but it's the only thing I own." Kelleigh rubbed at her eyes with her fingertips. Dennis's words rang in her ears. No transport. How the hell was she supposed to get around now?

"I truly am sorry. I'm out that way later on today so I can drop the paperwork in to start the full insurance claim. You're lucky you had insurance."

True. It was somewhat amazing that Rodrigo had used her money to actually pay a bill and not spent it all on going to some ritzy nightclub. The bank, if nothing else, would be happy with a repayment toward her debt. "How long does that take to process? And what's my car worth?" Numbness washed over her, but she had to think of the positives. She was going to sell the damn thing anyway.

"Er ... Miss. ... do you know anything about cars?"

"No, not really. My ex-boyfriend bought it brand new for me, about four years ago."

"Well, its logbook has never been completed so we can't verify if it's been serviced by an authorized repairer. Whoever did maintenance on it hasn't used genuine parts. And for a city car, the poor thing has done a lot of miles."

Kelleigh could feel her blood boil and she gritted her teeth together. Damn Rodrigo. He'd spend a thousand dollars on going out and having a good time, but not spend the money on servicing her car properly. What kind of man was he? He said he'd take care of everything. Yeah right! Her car obviously was not a priority. Neither was she, for that matter.

"What's the insurance going to pay out on it?"

"Twenty thousand."

"What? It's a freaking Mini Cooper. I was expecting more like thirty thousand."

"Miss Johnstone, I'm sorry. But with the damage and poor maintenance on the car, there's no way you're going to get any more than that. You're entitled to a second evaluation, of course, but in my experience you'd be wasting your time."

So much for getting out and about to see the sights of the Hunter Valley, or venturing to Sydney and Newcastle on the weekends. She couldn't do that in the company's hired Landcruiser, thanks to their strict policy on vehicle usage. She was stuck here in the middle of nowhere for three more weeks.

Ending the call with Dennis, she glared at her phone, wanting to crush it within her clenched fist and throw the remains against the wall, but instead she left it on the desk and opted for cursing, swearing and thrashing a cushion against the couch to vent some steam. Picturing Rodrigo's face as she slammed the pillow about made her feel better. There'd be no more keeping her frustrations locked up inside.

After her little outburst, she placed the cushion neatly back on the couch, flicked her hair out of her face and tied it back into place with a band. Calmly she walked over to the kitchenette and made a fresh cup of coffee in the Nespresso machine. Thank goodness for decent coffee, none of that instant crap. The deep, rich aroma and long sip placated her as she resumed her seat at the desk. Yes ... all better. Kelleigh had opened up the planning schedule on her laptop when her cell phone rang again. She grabbed it and rolled her eyes when she noted the caller ID. There may be more cushion bashing in a minute or two.

"Hi Kel, it's Toru. Settling in all right?" She rubbed the center of her forehead as she concentrated to understand his strong Asian accent. Toru Kei, five years her junior and her boss, seemed as useless as tits on a bull. He was the "yes" man, and she was quite convinced his sole purpose in his role was to suck up to the senior executives in Japan. Ever since she started working on this project, she'd already tried to pull him up on several things that were not technically possible in the designs for the resort. But he brushed her off with no regard to her input and assured her everything would be okay. His lack of engineering knowledge worried her and her stress levels, the headache-inducing kind, escalated every time the man was near.

"Yeah. All settled. I've met with Larry and the contractors. All systems are in place for us to start setting up this afternoon when the boys arrive with the drilling truck. Larry's also given us permission to leave the heavy equipment on-site."

"Excellent. You've done well." She heard him clear his throat loudly. That was never a good sign with him. "I fly up there first thing tomorrow morning. I've arranged meetings to discuss our project with some people and I'd like you to come with me so you can help outline the schedule. Our first meeting is tomorrow morning at eleven. Get the boys together and I'll take you all out to dinner tomorrow night. Okay? Yes?"

"I didn't know you planned on coming up so soon."

"I fly into Newcastle, then drive to Pokolbin. I will pick you up from your hotel. I will be there about ten-thirty. Okay, yes?"

"Is there anything I need to know for the meetings?"

"We have some exciting new developments. Yes."

Calling him the "yes" man was certainly apt, and she tried not to laugh. "What new developments have there been?"

"There is nothing for you to be concerned about."

"All right. I'll see you tomorrow."

She ended the call and replayed their conversation through her mind. She chewed on a broken fingernail as she stared at the laptop screen in front of her. For Toru to be heading up here earlier than expected there must be something major brewing. But what? He said don't worry, which of course now had her concocting up all sorts of scenarios. What developments could there be?

She grumbled as she noted the time on her watch. The morning was slipping away. When she'd met with Larry last week he hadn't been well, so this morning at breakfast she'd arranged with Grace to do up some soup and goodies for her to take out to him for lunch. He'd been so nice and helpful as she'd gone through all the legal documentation with him for approving access to his farm to run all the site tests and survey the land. Taking him a nice healthy meal, which he looked in desperate need of, was the least she could do before her team arrived.

She turned off the computer, slipped on her visibility vest, tied up her steel-caps, grabbed the rest of her gear and headed out the door.

***

"Larry? It's Kelleigh from JLR," she called out, knocking loudly on the screen door while balancing the takeaway cardboard tray overflowing with food in her other hand.

"What? Wait a minute." She heard a lot of shuffling and something crashing to the floor before footsteps headed toward her. "I thought you weren't going to be here until after lunch. You don't have to come and see me all the time. You can access the farm as you need. I thought I made that clear," Larry muttered as he came into view, tying up his dressing gown.

"I know. But I thought I would bring you some lunch. It's some vegetable soup, ham sandwiches and Grace was positive you wouldn't say no to custard tarts."

Larry looked like he had started salivating as he licked his lips. "Come on. Come on in. Damn Grace and her meddling. Got her nose in everywhere, hasn't she." He smiled, deep creases etching his face as he opened the door.

She followed him down the little hallway to the tiny old kitchen where they sat one week ago. The difference today was the pile of dirty dishes in the sink while empty tins of tomato soup and an old-looking loaf of bread littered the bench. She looked at Larry, trying to hide the concern on her face.

"You sit down, Larry, I'll get everything. Now, where are your plates, bowls and spoons?"

He waved weakly at a cupboard in the corner of the kitchen and she dived into a mixed array of chinaware. Nothing matched. She grabbed what was needed and set everything out on the table.

"My team from Melbourne should be here soon. We're going to start marking out the spots for drilling this afternoon up on the far hill and work our way down toward the creek."

"No worries. Jett's around here somewhere today. He's my farmhand. Did I already tell you that?" She nodded, he had—at least three times during their meeting last week. "Sorry he wasn't here when you visited, but he knows to help you if needed. He's going away this weekend for two weeks holiday. It will give you a chance to get all your testing done without any interference from the day-to-day farm operations for a while. The sooner you get what you need the better, so all this legal stuff can go through council for approval."

She couldn't agree more as she served out the food, glad to see Larry hook in to the meal. "Aren't you sad to sell this place? How long have you lived here?"

Larry hesitated, avoiding looking at her as he stirred the hot soup with his spoon. His voice lowered. "It's been in my family for three generations. But now, my kids don't want anything to do with it. They've all grown up and have to deal with their own lives and families. No one wants a cattle and small produce farm. What else could I do but sell? It's time to move on. All good things must come to an end."

"I'm so sorry, Larry. You should be happy knowing that the resort JLR have planned for this place is spectacular." However, bulldozing someone's legacy that had been passed down generation to generation and turning it into a multimillion-dollar golf course didn't seem right to her. Looking at Larry's weatherworn and drawn face tugged on her heart in a strange way. He was such a sweet man. "As our contract with you is conditional, what are you going to do when our application is approved and the sale is finalized? Where are you going to go?"

He closed his eyes, struggling to hide his emotions. "I'm planning to move to Coffs Harbour on the Central Coast, be near my sons and grandkids."

His words hung heavy on her heart. This man's livelihood was about to be taken away from him within a matter of months.

"It will be hard to see this place turned into a damn golf resort. If it has to be developed, I'd sooner see it as a golf course than covered in housing. I know I could have tried to sell it as a farm, but I didn't want to have to deal with scumbag real estate agents or pay them a fortune in commissions. When my lawyer approached me with your company's offer to buy the place, it sounded so nice and easy. I'm too old for drama these days."

She ate a couple of sandwiches, listening intently as Larry told her stories about growing up on the farm as a boy, his wife who died five years ago from nothing more than old age, and his kids and grandkids. His life, so full of happy treasured family memories. Maybe this wasn't a good idea to spend time with Larry. The more she got to know him, the more she cared about him and she couldn't afford to be emotionally invested. Every project she'd worked on in her past always seemed to upset someone. Crush someone's dreams. Shatter someone's livelihood. With this new job of hers she was supposed to be sitting in an office and avoiding face-to-face dealings with the customers, but here she was, out on-site chatting with the client over lunch. Pushing her plate away from her, she pinched the bridge of her nose and closed her eyes. It was time to focus on the tasks at hand. This place *was* to be torn down to nothing and sculpted into a grand eighteen-hole golf course. And it was her responsibility to make sure her feasibility studies were done on schedule to meet the project requirements. It was time to get off her backside, step outside and work.

Chapter 9

"I've arranged a meeting with several people while I'm here and we will present at the council meeting tomorrow night. Okay, yes?" Toru said to her after picking her up on Tuesday morning.

"Sure. Who are they with and why are we meeting with them?" she asked as she made herself comfortable in the passenger seat.

"One is with a farm owner behind Larry's, the other one is at Gumtrees Winery. The big bosses want us to talk to them about the resort and plans for future expansion."

"What future expansion?"

"We are nearly there. I'll explain everything during the meeting. Yes?"

The hairs on her arms prickled. Why was Toru skirting around her questions? The names Toru rattled off didn't mean anything to her. As Toru drove towards the dirt road leading up to Larry's farm and where she had her car crash, she couldn't help but think of Troy. She wondered where he was and what he was doing right now.

"Where are we going?" She sat up; concerned that Toru had

missed the turnoff. "I thought you said the meetings were with the property owners bordering Larry's; this place is on the other side of the road. Why are we meeting with this vineyard?"

Kelleigh's mouth gaped open when Toru drove through the grand sandstone gateway and up the long gravel driveway. She'd seen none of this the other day when she'd had her accident way down on the side road. A beautiful sandstone homestead, cellar door and restaurant, barns, quaint little cabins and a cottage, huge machinery and wine production sheds stood surrounded in all directions by the rolling hills covered in vibrant leafy grapevines. Everywhere she looked, the land was so green, painted every shade imaginable. It was one of the most magnificent places she'd ever seen.

"If you missed the sign on the gateway, this is Gumtrees Winery. We have a meeting with Nick Hill, the owner."

"But why? You still haven't explained." Kelleigh smoothed her hands over the legs of her dress pants as Toru pulled the car up outside the reception area. She hated meetings and her nerves were making her jittery.

"I told you, it's about our plans for the development. No need to repeat myself twice. You coming, yes?" Toru asked as he got out of the car.

Reluctantly she grabbed her laptop bag and stepped out of the car; her shoes wobbled on the graveled driveway surface. Give her a set of flats or steel-cap boots any day over the high-heeled pumps that graced her feet at the moment. Suits and fancy shoes were not her wardrobe of choice, but necessary for client meetings.

She glanced toward the front door; something drew her attention to the office area. An energy that lured her closer. It was warm, inviting and addictive. Unable to look away, she walked up the couple of steps toward the entrance, concentrating on putting one foot in front of the other so as not to trip and make a fool of herself in front of her boss.

A gush of air swooshed loudly when she pushed open the oak-colored timber door, and she followed Toru inside.

Holy shit!

She froze on the spot when she saw Troy sitting behind the desk.

What the hell was he doing here? The conversations she had with him flickered through her mind; he'd never enlightened her about his location of work. They'd agreed not to talk about work. There'd been no logos on his t-shirt, no names dropped, no mention of it.

"Kelleigh? What are you doing here?" He stood up so quickly from his chair it tipped over and crashed to the floor with a bang.

"You two know each other?" A man with mousey gray hair stood in the doorway behind Troy. His eyes darted from hers to Troy's like he was watching a tennis rally.

"No!" She said at the same time as Troy said, "Yes."

The man grinned and walked around to greet her and Toru with a firm handshake. "I'm Nick Hill and this is my business partner and co-owner, Troy Smith."

Business partner! Co-owner! Oh, this just gets better and better.

Kelleigh struggled to swallow the lump that had formed in her throat, her eyes unable to leave Troy's. This was not going to be an easy meeting, especially when all she could do was picture Troy in bed with her the other night in her hotel room. Her cheeks flushed and heat coursed along her neckline. She'd never felt so embarrassed and uncomfortable in all her life.

With Troy standing before her, the air around her felt electric and tingled her skin all over. She'd thought about Troy constantly, but never expected to see him again. Ever. This brought a whole new level of discomfort. A distraction was necessary to take her mind off those arms, those lips and those hands. Oh, and what was sheathed within his pants. The way Troy was looking at her, she couldn't quite work out whether he was trying to stab daggers through her or trying to undress her. Possibly a bit of both, but she certainly hoped for the latter.

Somehow she shoved her desire to seduce him again aside and found her voice. "Hello Nick, this is Mr. Toru Kei, general manager of JLR here in Australia. I'm Kelleigh Johnstone, engineering project leader."

"Excellent. Come on through to our office."

Kelleigh's knees wobbled as she followed the gentlemen through to one of the small offices tucked in behind the reception area. Awards and photos adorned the walls, while a large desk piled high with paperwork lay to one side of the room and a round table that could sit four people sat on the other. With sweating hands, she sat with Troy on her left. When her knees brushed against his as they pulled in their chairs, the smile he gave her sent a quiver straight between her legs.

Just her luck. Why did her one-night stand have to come back and haunt her? Troy's vivid blue eyes were even more accentuated by the sky-blue polo shirt emblazoned with the vineyard's logo on the breast pocket. He could have worn that the other day! She tried to resist the temptation, but gave in and scanned her eyes over his entire body as he sat next to her. Hopefully her actions were subtle. His ankles were crossed underneath the chair; his feet, adorned in RM Williams boots, jiggled away at a hundred miles an hour. Strong muscular thighs clad in faded denim jeans sat inches from her own legs. Then there were those arms. Muscular, well-toned biceps, perfectly sculpted, not over the top like a bodybuilder. The ones he had wrapped around her all night. Her heartbeat picked up a notch, remembering what a fine specimen he was underneath those clothes. All man in prime condition.

"Excuse me, would anyone like some tea or coffee?" A small plump woman ducked her head into the room.

"Ah, good timing. This is my lovely wife, Maria," Nick said as he settled in his seat next to Toru. "What shall we get you to drink?"

Maria took orders for coffee and tea, and then disappeared down the hallway.

"So how do you two know each other?" Nick waved his finger between herself and Troy.

Kelleigh cleared her throat and shuffled in her seat. "He helped me last week with my car when I had a flat tire." She surprised herself with how steady her voice remained.

Troy focused on his hands resting on the table before him. "And I saw her again at Harrigan's on Tuesday night."

"Oh." Nick's eyes widened and he chuckled. "*Oh!*"

Kelleigh's cheeks felt like they were on fire. Did Troy tell Nick about the other night? From the smirk on Nick's face and Troy's blushing cheeks, it was obvious he had.

Please earth, open up now and swallow me whole!

Maria returned with coffees, easing Kelleigh's embarrassment. After placing them on the table she promptly left.

"Mr. Kei, you wanted to discuss your company's plans in the region. While I'm interested in knowing what's going on in the area, what's this got to do with us?" Nick asked, before taking a sip from his cup.

"Thank you, Mr. Hill and Mr. Smith, for giving us the opportunity to meet with you. We have entered into an agreement to purchase Mr. Larry Peterson's property for the development of a golf course."

Kelleigh's stomach took a dive when the expression on the men's faces washed over with shock. Troy and Nick's mouths gaped open and they shook their heads in disbelief. "What did you say?" Troy blinked several times.

"We have started undertaking the necessary feasibility studies to submit a rezoning request and development application to council for approval in three weeks. Ms. Johnstone is our project leader and will be leading a small team to survey Mr. Peterson's property, coordinate audits and collect the required soil and water samples for testing. I will be here on and off during this period to meet with other people to ensure our application proceeds."

"I didn't even know Larry was interested in selling." Nick wiped his hand down across his drawn face.

"You can't build a resort on Larry's place. It's prime agricultural land. It's not possible, is it?" Troy looked gutted as he slumped back in his chair.

"We believe that the rezoning request will be approved based on other developments that have gone ahead in the area. More eco-friendly tourism and growth is part of this region's economic plan. We will be announcing our project at the general community and council meeting tomorrow night."

Kelleigh's skin prickled as the strain on Nick and Troy's faces became more evident as the minutes ticked by. Troy's knuckles had turned white from clenching his fists together. Releasing and stretching his fingers, he moved his hands underneath the table and rested them on top of his thighs.

Kelleigh's mind strayed. The thought of him, clutching her breasts with those strong hands while she clawed at the bed sheets when he made her come the other night had her biting down hard on her lip. When he slipped those firm fingers inside her and touched her in all the right places, he'd made her gasp for more. She shook her head. She shouldn't be thinking of stuff like this in the middle of a meeting. What was wrong with her? It was taking all her strength to not reach out and touch him; to feel his flesh again. She closed her eyes, trying to find composure, but the vision of his naked body was all she could see. His tongue circling her nipples. His shaft thrusting inside her. His skin sweating against hers. Her heartbeat started to escalate as she remembered how he felt against her during that night. *Holy hell, it was getting hot in here!* Her eyes shot open. Luckily no one seemed to notice she had been daydreaming. Which was ridiculous. She was a professional. She had to focus. She had a job to do.

"We have grand plans for this development." Toru continued. "We'd like to show you the initial design plans because there are other matters we need to discuss. Ms. Johnstone will also show you details of the studies we will be conducting." He waved at Kelleigh to open up her laptop.

Kelleigh fumbled with her computer, then awkwardly clambered down around behind her chair to plug the cord into power because the battery was running low. All the while she sensed Troy's eyes boring in to her. With him watching her every move, he made her aware of her entire being—of the way her silk blouse felt cool across her skin, how her hair brushed softly against her back when she moved and how he made the blood swirl through her veins. No other man had ever made her feel her like that. Troy took a long slow sip of his drink, and as he put the cup down on the table he wiped his thumb back and forth across his bottom lip. Her inner core clenched and her throat ran dry, knowing what that mouth could do.

Troy and Nick nodded at appropriate times as she went through the feasibility study schedule—there was nothing unusual about it. It was considerate to let them know what was going on and not be concerned when all the trucks and contractors visited Larry's place over the coming weeks. Then Toru spun her laptop around to face him, plugged in his USB and started his own slideshow, showing off the designs for the multimillion-dollar golf resort.

Her eyes bulged as he went through each slide. The presentation had changed. The plans had been modified since she'd seen them a few weeks ago. Why hadn't she'd been told that the development had grown? Now there was a new conference center and more residential villas. Where had this come from?

"But this development won't fit on Larry's place. His land is only one hundred acres," Troy noted, looking closely at the overall map.

"You are correct." Toru said, "The size of our desired project brings us to the reason for this meeting. JLR's vision is a fully integrated tourism facility; therefore we'd like to explore the opportunity to purchase your land as well. We've done some preliminary investigations and would be willing to offer you a significant sum for its acquisition."

Kelleigh's mouth jerked open, her head flew around and she glared at Toru. This had never been part of the plan. How dare he not talk to her about this before the meeting? Her gut felt like it had been kicked. She was embarrassed and pissed off at not being included in management's circle of information. She was the project leader on-site and should have been informed.

Colleagues had told her previously Toru was ruthless in negotiations and often won; she'd hate to see this beautiful vineyard destroyed for their development. But what could she do? She had to go along with her company's plans. She wasn't in a position to do anything else. She lowered her eyes and stared at her coffee cup to hide her disappointment. Days like this, she absolutely hated her job.

"Gumtrees is not for sale." Both men said in unison.

"We have our own expansion plans in place that are already approved by council." Nick looked like he couldn't believe what he was hearing. "There's no amount of money on this planet you could offer us to make us sell. Thank you, but no thank you."

"Money talks, Mr. Hill." Toru looked smug in his seat, even had a glint in his eye. "The offer would be very substantial. You potentially could retire and never have to work another hard day in your life."

"Gumtrees is not for sale." Troy repeated. Kelleigh shied away from the hatred radiating off his skin. She didn't know what to say or do to ease the growing tension between the men; she herself was still in shock.

Toru delved into his folder and pulled out some papers. "I have a document here for you outlining our proposed plans, and a confidentially agreement for you to sign if you wish to enter negotiations."

"Won't be necessary." Nick didn't even touch the file when Toru placed it on the desk and Troy folded his arms defensively across in front of him.

"We're not for sale. That's final," Troy leaned back in his chair. "We don't want some ghastly accommodation complex creating an eyesore in our Valley."

"I can assure you it won't be an eyesore." Kelleigh tried to put them at ease. "I've worked on this project with the architects and can assure you it will be a five-star eco-friendly design."

Troy leaned forward, his piercing blue eyes narrowed into sharp dagger-like slits. "We'll do everything in our power to stop this from proceeding. This is outrageous. There are enough resorts and golf courses in this area already. We don't need another one."

"We don't see any issues with our application being approved by council." Toru remained nonchalant, steepling his fingertips in front of his chest. "This development will proceed with or without our acquisition of your property."

Troy and Nick's shoulders sagged, as if burdened with heavy weight.

"We'll see about that," Troy said through his strained jaw.

Nick stood up, his chair scraping loudly against the sandstone-tiled floor. "I think we're done here."

"Thank you for your time, gentlemen," Toru stood up and offered his hand, which the men reluctantly shook.

Troy's eyes, filled with disappointment and hurt, flicked her way before he departed from the office without a word. Nick was left standing there with her and Toru. So much for friendly farewells.

"Before we depart, Mr. Hill, may I please use your restroom?" Toru asked as he gathered his folders.

"Sure, it's down the hallway, third door on the left."

Kelleigh agreed to wait for Toru at the car before he excused himself. Nick led her back out through the reception area and bid her goodbye. As she walked outside, the searing hot sunshine hitting her face was a welcome relief; so much better than the icy-cold glares and tension that had filled the room during the meeting.

That had been the worst meeting in her life. What Toru did was very unprofessional. She was embarrassed not knowing the full meeting's agenda. If she had the nerve she'd give him a piece of her mind. She shook herself free of the negative vibe as she walked toward the car, but her head spun back around toward the doorway when she heard her name being called.

Great. This was not what she needed.

"Kelleigh. Wait!" Troy jammed his Akubra hat onto his head, looking very much like Tom Burlinson in *The Man From Snowy River.* But anger flared in his eyes and his jaw was clenched as he stormed toward. Her dreamy image of him dissipated in a puff of smoke. "What the hell was that? You knew about this and didn't tell me."

Her mouth opened in shock at his accusation. "Tell you what? About the development? I couldn't say anything because there was a confidentiality agreement in place."

"What a load of hogwash. Was this part of some sick plan? Did you think that by sleeping with me I'd willingly give you Gumtrees?"

She took a step back at his harsh words. "Never! I'd never do such a thing. I didn't know you worked here. You never told me *where* you worked."

His eyes flickered, maybe trying to recall their conversations. "Are you sure about that?"

"Positive. You never mentioned you worked at Gumtrees. And what Toru said came as a surprise to me as well. He mentioned there'd been some changes but wouldn't elaborate on the details even when I asked. I swear I had no idea JLR wanted to buy this place. That was not part of the original plan." Her voice trembled as she spoke. She didn't want him to be angry with her and couldn't have him thinking she was deceptive.

"That sounds hard to believe," he said through tightened lips, the veins on the side of his neck bulged. "Regardless of what happened between us last week, it will not sway my decision in any way. You will not get your hands on this place. Understand?"

Kelleigh glared, momentarily lost for words. If this was the way he reacted to things that upset him, she wondered about his true nature. "And you must understand I had no idea who you were and didn't think I'd ever see you again," her voice assertive in her defense.

"Well, surprise, here I am."

"Look, I'm here to do my job. I'm not involved with acquisitions." How had she landed in the middle of all this stressful mess?

"Fine." His sapphire eyes flared beneath the rim of his hat and his fists clenched by his sides. "I give you fair warning, you'll be hearing from our lawyers. We will be doing everything possible to ensure that this development doesn't proceed."

As she held her ground, she gave him a comprehending nod.

"Good day then, Miss Johnstone." He dipped his head before he turned on the heel of his boots and headed in the direction of the work sheds.

She let out a deep breath, it seemed like she'd been holding on to for an eternity. Her hands trembled as she ran her fingers through her hair and fought back the sting in her eyes. Troy had looked at her with such contempt. No longer heated desire. One of the best nights of just-for-the fun-of-it, let-off-some-steam, fuck-everything-in-the-world, crazy, fun sex now made her feel terrible. She dropped her head back and stared at the vast expanse of blue sky above. "Haven't I got enough crap to deal with?"

Then she thought of Fran and Jamie. Jamie was still trying to find work every day and their baby due in a short number of weeks. Okay, Kelleigh had her debts, her problems; a horrid boss, but this job would pay her bills. That's right, she had to think of the positives. As limited as they may be.

"Kelleigh? Come on, it's time for our next meeting." Toru skipped down the stairs and opened his car door. "Let's go."

She forced a smile, reluctantly slid into the passenger seat and buckled up. Her own frustration rippled through her veins. She hated Troy being upset with her, but Toru's behavior irked her even more. She twisted her hands into knots. She was not one to question management's decisions, but going into an important meeting without all the facts was not fair. "Why didn't you tell me on the way out here that the plans had changed? That was embarrassing, not knowing the big picture."

"It was irrelevant. You only needed to show the plans for the feasibility studies."

She crossed her arms and stared out the passenger window. Any respectable person would have informed her of such changes and not lead her into a meeting blind. What was he playing at? Trying to make her look incompetent? That infuriated her even further. She couldn't wait to get this job over and done with, get her bags packed and leave this town once and for all.

Chapter 10

The next morning Troy pulled his Cruiser up outside Larry's old farmhouse, grabbed the paper bag full of pastries off the seat next to him and headed up the stairs. Maria's cooking smelled delicious and he started to salivate, eager to have a taste. But checking up on Larry was not the only reason for his visit, Troy wanted to get to the bottom of this deal he had with JLR. Why would Larry sell without mentioning it?

"Hello," he called out, and knocked on the screen door.

"Troy, that you?" Larry's voice came from within the depths of the house. "Come on in, the door is unlocked. You're just in time for a cuppa."

The screen door creaked open and shut with a bang behind him. He walked into the kitchen, placed the bag on the table and threw his hat down beside it.

"Sounds good. I stole some of Maria's pastries. I know how much of a sweet tooth you have."

"That I do, young man. That I do. They'll go well with the pot of tea I was about to make."

"Here, you take a seat and I'll make the tea." Troy pulled

back a chair from the table and insisted Larry take a seat.

"I guess I know the reason for your visit." Larry mumbled. "You've finally heard about me wanting to sell the place."

Troy paused momentarily before scooping more tealeaves into the kettle and poured boiling water on top.

"Why didn't you tell us? You should have talked to Nick and me. There's maybe something we could have done."

Larry's sunken cheeks drew into a sullen smile. "Maybe. Maybe not. You don't need to worry yourselves with my problems. But when I was sick this past winter and needed to get my affairs into order, my lawyer suggested this development to me. His firm represents JLR here in Australia and it sounded like an easy option. Not having to deal with scumbag real estate agents or pay the bastards all that commission for no work. Nope. This resort mob offered me a great price on the proviso that the application is approved. They seem very confident or they wouldn't be here, right?"

"Right." Troy's voice trailed off while he poured the tea and stirred in milk. Seeing this place turned into a resort would be such a waste of prime farmland. He could understand why JLR wanted it so badly. The rolling foothills, the endless green pastures, rich soil and running creek was a definite drawcard.

"They visited us yesterday and proposed to buy Gumtrees as well. Nick and I, of course, wouldn't have a bar of it. I think they'll have the same, if not more colorful opposition from Brian up the road. They went to see him after us." Troy placed the tea down in front of Larry and sat down opposite him.

"What? It's only supposed to be my place." Larry shook his head. "I'm sorry, kid. This is wrong. I didn't know they had bigger plans."

"They won't if I have anything to do with it." Troy held the cup to his lips over the rim to cool the contents down. "So what are you going to do with yourself, old man?"

"Retire. I'm eighty years old and still working the land. I can't do it anymore. My bones aren't as young as yours. I'm going to move to Coffs Harbour to be near my kids and grandkids."

"You're moving away? But this is your home." Larry was a good friend and it would be sad to see him leave the district.

"If this sale goes through, it won't be for much longer. Jett's upset, but he's young and will find another job. He's a good kid and I hated having to tell him. He's agreed to stay on until the development plan is approved. Maybe one thing you could do after all this is finalized is offer him a job. I know Nick's been talking about hiring more hands, especially coming up to harvest."

"Geez, I don't know, Larry." Jett was a great farmhand, but he didn't think he could afford two full-time staff. During harvest, yes. But long-term was a different story. "I'll have to wait and see. You remember my son, Conner, I offered him a job and I'm waiting to see what he wants to do."

Larry slowly nodded his head. "I understand."

"Nick and I really don't want this development to go ahead. I can't see Brian agreeing to this and I don't know about Bill on the other side of you, but is there any way we can stop this? Is there anything in the contract that gives you an out? I'm sorry if it's not going to be what you want, but I have to think of the surrounding farmland and the effect it will have on us around here."

Larry's shoulders slouched. "I thought as much. I hoped this was going to be an easy process, but I guess that's not going to happen. You young things have so much fight in you; I wish I had it in me. I see now that I should have talked to you first."

"Are you sure there's no clause in your agreement?"

"Hold on a sec." Larry slowly pushed back from his chair and walked out into the other room. Troy heard the floorboards creak under his footsteps, the drawer of a filing cabinet sliding in and out and the rustling of paper before he returned with a pile of documents and red A4-sized books.

"What's all this?" Troy asked as Larry placed the pile down in front of him.

"This is a copy of the agreement." The old man's gnarled-knuckled finger pointed to the document on the top. "And these are all my account books for the past three years. Maybe you can take a look at them for me and tell me what you think the place is worth, because if by some slim chance this development doesn't proceed, I'm still going to have to sell up. I'd hate to see some city slicker buy the place for their weekend getaway and let the land go to waste."

"A golf course is worse. They'll sculpt the land, knock down the trees, change the waterways and build ugly villas everywhere. I know which one I'd prefer." Troy grunted as he bit into a pastry.

Larry groaned as he sat slowly back down on his chair. "This was supposed to be an easy solution. A quick way out so I can move on. You do what you must and I'll help you out with anything I know. It's good to see you have the spirit to fight."

"And I'll do everything possible to ensure I win." This land meant a lot to him; it was in his blood. He wasn't going to see it developed into some hideous golf course without putting up his best efforts to stop them. "Thanks for all this, Larry, but I better get going now. The council meeting is on tonight and I need to finish off the spraying before I clean up and head into Harrigan's. You want to come?"

"Nope. I'm going to stay well away from the firing squad. You can tell me all about it later." Larry winked at him as he slurped on his hot cup of tea. "Have you met the young lass, Kelleigh? She is one tough lass, heading up the team of boys here on-site."

"Humph! Yes, I've met her." Troy gathered the plates and rinsed them off at the sink to avoid Larry seeing the heat rise up his neck at the mention of her name. "She came to the meeting at Gumtrees yesterday. Wouldn't have picked her as a project leader." Kelleigh consumed his mind for most of his waking hours since he'd met her on the side of the road and spending the night with her last week. But everything changed now he knew who she was. She'd lied to him and deceived him. When she walked into the office, he nearly tripped over himself. He'd been toying with the idea of going to Harrigan's again and hopefully … accidentally … run into her again, but instead, she ended up on his doorstep. For the first half of the meeting he couldn't believe his luck at seeing her again and having the chance to maybe hook up again while she was in town. But now, that notion had truly disappeared. It was his mission in life to see her and her company sent on their way, out of the Hunter Valley for good.

"Pity we don't get fine lasses like that coming to live around this town anymore."

"She won't be here for long if I have anything to do with it." He noticed a twinge of disappointment in the depths of his chest as he spoke those words. That instant attraction he felt for Kelleigh when he saw her stranded by the road; that intense chemistry he felt when he flirted with her over drinks and the insane, hot passion between them when in her bedroom was something he hadn't felt in a long time. Pity it was so short-lived.

Now he knew who Kelleigh was and things were put into perspective, there'd be no more crazy, lustful thoughts about her. Enough was enough. Returning to Larry's table, he gathered up all the documents, notebooks and his hat. He had to think about Gumtrees. He glanced at the clock; time was getting away from him yet again. "I have to get going. Those vines aren't going to spray themselves." He hooked the load of books under his arm. "Thanks for this. It means a lot. I'll let you know if I find anything and will have a chat with our lawyers. We'll chat soon."

Troy tipped the rim of his hat, scooted down the hallway, jumped in his Cruiser and headed back to Gumtrees. He wasn't a lawyer, he wasn't an accountant but he was good at math. First thing he'd do before heading out in the field was call Maxine, Jessica's best friend, who was a corporate mergers and acquisitions lawyer. At least, she might be able to give him some points in the right direction on how the hell he could stop this development from proceeding.

Chapter 11

Harrigan's was overflowing with locals waiting for the council meeting to commence at five o'clock in the afternoon. Conversations filled the air around Troy, who sat at the bar talking to Brian and a couple of other men about the JLR project. No point in keeping it secret any longer. Brian, the grumpy ol' bugger, was about as impressed as Troy and Nick had been when he heard the plans from Kelleigh and Toru.

"Threatened to get my shotgun out if they didn't get off my property quick smart," Brian smirked.

Troy hesitated, eyeing off the man wondering if he would carry out such a serious threat. In fact, the more he thought about, Brian probably would.

As Troy listened intently and more people joined in his discussion, his confidence grew quietly as support gathered to stop the project. But he couldn't ignore the disappointment at his conduct toward Kelleigh after the meeting yesterday. She wasn't the one to blame. He was not like that. He rarely lost his temper, but the threat made against his home and livelihood had sent rage shooting through his veins like a dragster thundering down the track.

He scratched at his chin. He didn't want her thinking he was an ogre. After the meeting tonight he would make the effort to find her here at Harrigan's and apologize.

"Come on. We'd better get into this meeting and see what we can do to stop this project." Troy slid off the bar stool, grabbed his glass of beer and headed down the short corridor to the large meeting room at the back of Harrigan's. The hair on his arms stood on end as he walked past the hallway that led down to the guest rooms. Why was he so on edge? Surely not because of Kelleigh?

An uncomfortable niggle grew at the base of his neck when he entered the crowded room. Loud chatter bombarded his ears, but his attention was drawn to the desks at the front. His gaze darted around the milling people to see what the drawcard was. As he shuffled past some guests, the way cleared before him. Knots pulled tight like a winch in his stomach, stopping him in his tracks when he caught sight of her. As if sensing his presence, she looked up at him. Her green eyes pierced into his.

Kelleigh.

What was she doing here? He quickly scanned the room; he thought Toru was supposed to be here, not her.

Noting the time on the far wall, he had five minutes until the meeting commenced. This was his opportunity to apologize now rather than later. Get it over and done with. He forced his reluctant feet to carry him forward.

She dismissed his approach, leaning down to point to something on the paper in front of the man sitting at the table.

"Evening," he said, stopping a short distance away. A few deep breaths didn't help settle his stomach.

She slowly stood upright and straightened her shoulders. "Hello Mr. Smith. What are you doing here?"

"I always attend the council community meetings. More

importantly, what are you doing here?" He raised a questioning eyebrow. "I thought Toru was attending tonight."

"He had to go back to Melbourne for an urgent meeting with some investors, so I'm going to do the presentation tonight."

Her voice shook with nerves and her forehead drew with furrows as her eyes darted around the room.

Troy watched her every move as she fumbled with the collar of her blouse. Maybe she hadn't had a lot of experience talking in front of a crowd, and he could sympathize with that, but having her around to charm the locals wouldn't sway things easily his way. It was going to make it even more difficult to rally the community behind him to stop the proposed development. There were many pro-development people in the area and Kelleigh, with her attractive looks and stunning smile, would quickly win over their shallow hearts.

"About yesterday." Troy struggled to find the right words. "I want to apologize for my behavior after our meeting. It was uncalled for and believe it or not, very out of character for me. I'm truly sorry. I didn't mean to upset you."

"Thank you. Apology accepted."

He put out his hand for her to shake, and as her hand slipped in to his a jolt of electricity coursed throughout his body. Heat, desire and want for her overwhelmed his senses. He wanted to drag her into his arms. Hug her. Kiss her. Feel her naked body next to his and breathe in her delicious scent. Images of them entwined together filled his mind bringing a smile to his face.

"Now, if you'll excuse me. I have to get ready for the meeting." Kelleigh said as he reluctantly let go of her hand.

A loud bang of a wooden hammer on the end of the table brought the room to attention and him back to reality. He was here to save Larry's place, rally community support and find a way to stop JLR's project from proceeding.

"Might see you after the meeting," Kelleigh whispered to

him while gathering up her documents. He was about to walk away but hesitated when he caught sight of a playful sparkle in her eyes, just like the one she had on the first night he met her in the pub. Baffled, he turned and walked to the back to the room to take a seat, struggling as the warm rush of blood through his veins made him falter in his steps. How could Kelleigh make him react this way when he opposed everything she and her company aimed to do?

While listening to the council's meeting, he couldn't draw his eyes away from Kelleigh. He barely took note of the speakers outlining new developments, infrastructure upgrades, and covered budgets before she presented to the group. Every word Kelleigh spoke had Troy clenching his fists in anger yet his groin niggling with desire. It was absurd. Absurd that he kept thinking about taking her down the hallway back to her room. Absurd that he wanted to make love to her again. Absurd that she affected him so. He hadn't been full of foolish thoughts over a woman in such a long time and now was definitely not the right time. It had to stop.

On conclusion of her presentation, the response jittering around the room was as he predicted. There was much chatter and divided opinion; some heated voices, some of praise. Her gaze found his; she smiled, looking relieved that it was all over. But for him this was just the beginning. He leaned back in his chair and folded his arms. Kelleigh remained at the front of the room, looking every bit confident and in control. There were no sign of nerves at all. Oh yes, with him fighting against her company to stop the project and now also fighting off his attraction toward her, he was in for one hell of an interesting battle ahead.

***

After the meeting concluded, Troy mingled though the locals gathering support against the development and started a partition for people to sign. It wasn't much, but it was something. At least one small step in the right direction.

All the while, he could sense Kelleigh and her movements wherever she was within the room. Like she was the eye of the cyclone and everything she did drew his attention toward her, dragging him closer and closer. Every time she looked his way. Every time she smiled. Every time she laughed. He ruffled his hands through his hair, frustrated. This floodgate of emotion had to be turned off because he would not get involved with someone who essentially was working for the enemy.

Everyone meandered out to the main bar for one last drink before heading home. After finishing his beer, he placed his empty glass on the counter and started to say his goodbyes when he heard angry voices splintering the air over in the far corner.

"You can take your bloody money and shove it where the sun don't shine, lovey." Brian's voice boomed at Kelleigh. She flinched at every word as he pointed his finger close to her face. "We don't need your stupid Japanese resort in this town. I never want to see you or any of your cronies near my land again. Do you hear me?"

Brian's face was bright red and his voice spit with rage. Regardless of his disapproval and resentment at what JLR aimed to do in their region, this was no way for Brian to talk to Kelleigh. With several quick strides he pushed through the crowd and made his way over to stand beside her.

"Are you okay?" he asked. She nodded but trembled all over.

"We don't need another damn golf course, Troy." Brian now pointed in his direction. "Don't you go defending this scum."

"Brian, it's okay. We'll sort this out, but going off at Kelleigh is not going to help the situation." God, he sounded like a hypocrite. He'd reacted in exactly the same manner. "How about I give you a lift home?" Troy held out his palm to guide Brian away from Kelleigh.

Brian rolled his shoulder, shrugging off Troy's offer. "I don't need your help, boy. I'm perfectly capable of looking after myself." Brian took a step closer toward him and thrust his finger near his face again. "You do whatever it takes to get this woman and her shitty resort out of our Valley. You hear me?"

"You know I will, but you don't need to talk to her like this. Have some respect."

"Respect? People like this don't deserve respect. She's the devil in disguise, I tell you." Brian's bloodshot eyes flared, as did his nostrils.

"Enough, Brian. Get out of here now, or I'll throw you out myself."

Brian sucked air in to his lungs loudly and puffed out his chest. Somewhere in the madness of the man's mind, sense took hold of him. He raised his hands up in surrender, turned and stormed out of the pub.

Troy eased around to face Kelleigh. Her face was drained of color. "He was getting a bit feisty, wasn't he?" Her voice trembled.

"Are you sure you're all right?" Troy went to put his hand on her arm, but stopped halfway. The thought of touching her bare skin played havoc on his mind because she was no longer nobody. No longer a one-night encounter. She'd become somebody and he didn't like the reason why she was in town. Her confrontation with Brian was a firm reminder. But regardless of their differences, he didn't tolerate Brian's bad behavior. Unlike Brian, Troy's behavior had not been normal. "Seems like we're both adamant about not selling. Like Larry, his place has been in his family for generations and I can't see he'd ever give it up. Not even over his dead body."

Kelleigh's shoulders slumped. Color slowly returned to her cheeks. Troy's skin still prickled from all the tension resonating in the air, even after Brian left. He quickly surveyed the remaining people in the room, all of them eyeing him and Kelleigh suspiciously. Were they waiting to have their own unfriendly word with her? He may be sitting on the opposite side of the fence to her on this project development, but people didn't need to be hostile toward her. He knew there were proper channels to go through for this dispute, rather than vent their anger and disappointment directly at her.

Here he was trying to protect her from the masses when there had been no one around to ward off his verbal attack on her. Nothing could undo how bad he felt about his actions. Hopefully, tonight Kelleigh could see he wasn't a brute and neither were these people. But for now, he had to get her out of here.

"Would you like to go for a walk outside? Get some fresh air and avoid this mob." He jutted his chin in the direction of the front door.

"Um ..." She mumbled as she rubbed her hand on her arm.

"It's a warm evening and the gardens should be really nice at sunset."

Kelleigh's nose wrinkled. "What gardens? The ones outside the pub?"

"No, the Hunter Valley Gardens on the other side of the roadway here." He pointed off to the side of Harrigan's.

"I've been so cooped up in my room working I haven't had a chance to see them yet."

"Come on. I'll show you." He gestured to the door again.

Her eyes fell from his to stare down at some spot on the floor. There it was, that hesitation. That moment of doubt. She was going to turn him down. With everything that had gone on between the two of them, he would understand if she said no.

Deep down he knew she would be right. He should stay away from her. He didn't trust her. Not one little bit. How could she not have known the full extent of the project her company envisaged for the area? He didn't buy her story at all. Yet here he was asking her for a walk. Was he asking for more trouble for himself? But the compulsion to make sure she was okay after tonight's hostilities was too overpowering to ignore.

"I might not be the best of company." Kelleigh swept her hair back and tucked it behind her ear.

"A walk in the fresh air might do us both some good." Yes, it would be good to put his mind at ease. "You got some better shoes than those?" He questioned, pointing to her high heels.

"Yes, I do. I need to get these damn things off my feet. They're killing me." She pointed her toe out in front of her and rolled her ankle around in tiny circles. "A walk sounds wonderful. I'll drop my gear off back in my room and change my shoes. Give me a minute?"

Kelleigh hooked her laptop bag over her shoulder and gathered up a huge pile of folders, from the nearby table. Struggling with the load, she started to head for her room.

"Let me help you with that." Troy eased her load and carried the folders for her.

The smile that played at the corner of her mouth made it all worthwhile. "This way," she said, heading down the hallway.

"I think I remember the way."

Chapter 12

In her room, Troy leaned against the doorjamb and watched her lace on her running shoes. He glanced at the wall mirror and then at the bed. His mind filled with the arousing images of taking off her clothes and all that went on here the other night.

To avoid his blood rushing south, he drew his gaze to elsewhere in the room. Kelleigh's work boots, covered in mud, lay beside the door. Her hi-vis clothing was piled in a heap on the ground before the bathroom door. Paperwork and maps lay across her desk. He grinned, liking her casual, unkempt nature.

"I'm ready." She stood up and tied her hair back with a band. She'd look stunning in anything, but clothed in dress pants, button-up blouse and running shoes was a sight to behold, making it hard for him to look away. Tucking his shirt into his jeans, checking his cell phone for emails and pulling up his socks offered little distraction from admiring her as he guided her outside the complex, up the roadway and onto the dirt pathway that led into the gardens.

"I can't believe you haven't been over here yet." Troy chided. "The Hunter Valley Gardens are one of the biggest tourist attractions in the area." He slowed his pace down so she could keep up. As they broke through the pocket of trees behind the row of nursery sheds, he heard Kelleigh gasp when she came in to view of the majestic gardens before them.

"They look spectacular."

"You shouldn't spend so much time in your bedroom. Not that I'd be complaining about that."

She smiled, nudging him gently in the side with her elbow, and continued down the path toward the lake, the sandy chitters crunching under each step.

"Wow. This place is huge." She looked around, taking in the manicured landscape before her.

"Yep. Over there is the Japanese Garden; that way is the Rose and Sunken Gardens. Up that way is the Storybook Garden, but let's head down this way to the Lakes Walk."

He placed her hand on the small of her back to direct her down the path, enjoying the moment of contact with her body. She glanced his way, causing his heartbeat to go up a notch. Why was he always attracted to the wrong type of woman? She seemed too much of a city girl, too mysterious and untrustworthy. And ultimately too temporary to consider anything else. So why did he find her more intriguing with each passing moment?

His palms started to go clammy and he struggled to withdraw his hand from touching her. He felt awkward and unsure of himself, just like on a first date. But his reality was he hadn't dated anyone in years. A few women in the Napa Valley never went beyond a dinner or two. The brief encounters with harvest workers, festival-goers or women he'd meet at the pub were all a bit of fun. Nothing serious. Nothing with any intent of longevity. Kelleigh, of course, fell into the one-night-only category and he needed to leave it at that. Dating wasn't an option for him. Not with her, not with anyone. There was no room in his life at the moment and he didn't have the time. Gumtrees was his focus.

"You were right, I needed some fresh air. I've had some pretty awful days since being here, it's nice to get outside and clear my head." Kelleigh tucked her hands into her pockets as she meandered along the track. "This project has certainly gone all crazy on me. I've only been with JLR for three months and I hate being dragged into all these meetings and presentations. It's usually not my role; it's all been rather stressful and I hate upsetting people."

"You've done a fine job at putting half the community against you and your company with this proposed development." He was definitely on the list.

"My problem is I take it personally." Venting her frustrations, she started to count out points on her fingers. "I hate upsetting people that will be affected by projects. I'm no good in meetings because I get so nervous I feel ill. I hate spending so much time in front of a computer responding to corporate communications. And while I do enjoy the design and construction side of engineering, I'd rather be out on-site all the time getting my hands dirty, drilling and surveying. Being project leader here gives me that chance to supervise all that, which is cool. Give me steel-caps and a pair of old jeans any day."

Her response caught him off guard. He thought she handled herself brilliantly. Looks could be so deceiving. Maybe she wasn't such a city girl after all.

With Kelleigh walking along beside him and staring at the ground, it made him think about his own path in life. From high school part-time work here in the Hunter Valley during harvest, to working in the US in Texas on a ranch, to the Napa Valley vineyards to Gumtrees. He'd never been the ambitious type. He was more the wherever-I-lay-my-hat-that's-my-home type of guy. He'd never been one to chase high incomes or prestige.

He was more about doing what he loved. It wasn't until after Nicola's death he listened to his heart and found his passion in viticulture. Going by the improvements he'd made at Gumtrees, he certainly had a knack for it.

"I can't even contemplate a career change at the moment, "she continued, "because my ex left me with a debt and I need the income to pay it off. Maybe in a few years I might consider a change." Her tone was a mix of anger, hurt, frustration and disappointment.

As they continued along the path past the rose beds, the sun started to set slowly in the west. Streaks of orange clouds glowed brightly on the distant horizon. It was Troy's favorite time of the day as he took in the heavens above. In the serenity of the evening falling and the crickets chirping loudly, Troy wanted to forget everything that had happened in the past couple of days. Forget about his meeting with her and Toru, forget about the council community meeting and Brian and forget about why Kelleigh was in town.

He paused beside one of the flowerbeds and scanned through the rosebushes. "Ah-ha!" He found what he was looking for, stepped in among the scrubs and carefully snapped off the bloom. How lucky he was to find one so late in the season. Pleased with himself, he stepped over toward Kelleigh who had stopped to wait for him and handed it to her.

Kelleigh froze. Her eyes widened and her arms tensed by her side. "What are you doing? You can't pick the flowers in here."

He ignored her concern and offered it to her. Her large emerald eyes glistened in the softening light while her hair danced in the gentle breeze. She looked radiant and it was starting to affect his pulse. "You faced a tough crowd tonight and we've had our own share of ... interesting meetings, so I'd like to call a truce. Please accept this as a peace offering."

From the look she gave him, she really did think he was an idiot.

"Are you serious?"

"Yes, please take the rose." She hesitated before taking the bloom carefully between her fingers to avoid the thorny stem. Holding it up to her nose, her eyes fluttered shut and her mood instantly transformed a she smelled its fragrant perfume.

Yes, he'd achieved his desired outcome; a smile. In spite of their opposition, he couldn't deny how attractive she was. Being alone with her in this intimate setting was maybe not such a good idea, because his body was starting to react of its own accord.

"That ... is the most amazing rose I've ever smelled." She said, intoxicated by the rose's scent.

"Pretty good, isn't it?" He liked to think she was impressed. "We have this same species of rose growing at the end of the trellises at Gumtrees. They help us monitor the health of the vines. Roses are susceptible to disease, so if they get sick it's a warning sign for us to act quickly before the vines are damaged."

"You're full of interesting facts, aren't you?" she said with a hint of sarcasm. "Pity they can't warn us about problems in real life." She stared at the rose in her hand.

"I don't know about that. Every time I'm around you alarm bells go off in my head." He stepped toward her. "I should stay away from you but somehow always seem to end up crossing your path. Why is that? I can't deny you certainly have me intrigued." His heartbeat started to escalate while looking at her. He should leave now. Walk away. But his legs wouldn't cooperate and held him firmly on the spot. He couldn't deny she was exquisite.

With trembling hands, he stepped closer, cupped her face with his hands and kissed her. Her sweet lips against his again. Those alarm bells were clanging inside his head. So loud they'd wake up an entire town. Coming for a walk was a bad idea. Being around her filled him with want. Thoughts of Kelleigh had rattled his brain for far too long. His will power to keep his distance had gone; desire had taken its place.

But she didn't respond in the way he expected. His brow furrowed when her lips tensed and turned hard like stone. Her hands planted firmly on the center of his chest and pushed him back with brute force. Before he could do anything, her hand flew through the air with a whoosh and slapped him hard, right on the cheek. It stung like hell and made his eyes water.

Blinking from shock and trying to ease the pain, he rubbed at the side of his face while Kelleigh glared at him with raging eyes.

"What the hell are you doing? How dare you?" she snapped.

"I'm sorry. I didn't mean to upset you."

"It's a bit late for that! I agreed to come for a walk with you. I was not leading you on or giving you an invitation to another romp in my bed. Do you think after everything that's happened I'd want to be with you again?"

"I said I'm sorry. I got caught up in the moment." How could he have been so stupid? This was the confirmation he needed to put a stop to all his crazy thoughts. Finally all his senses realigned. There would be no more confusion, flirtations or playful glances. And definitely no more peace offerings. He was done. From now on, he'd keep clear.

She huffed, pushed past him, chucked the rose into the garden bed and stormed off, back up the pathway to Harrigan's.

Shaking his head in disbelief, he started off after her to ensure she made it back to the hotel safely. There was no way he would ever make this mistake again.

As he rounded the corner of the building moments after Kelleigh, she turned to face him. Her shoulders pulled back tightly. Her mouth drawn into a tight line. Yep, she was still furious. It had not been his intention at all.

She inhaled sharply. "Thank you for helping me with Brian tonight. But after everything that has happened, the work I have to do and your goal to stop our project, I think it would be wise not to see each other again while I'm here. I'm sure you agree it's for the best."

Kelleigh avoided looking directly at him, but he was glad she'd drawn the same conclusion. He hated seeing her upset after trying to kiss her, but he wasn't going to waste any more of his time and effort. It was a lost cause.

"Sounds like a plan."

As he turned to leave, her hand grabbed his forearm and his heart jumped in his chest. For a moment he thought she'd changed her mind, and he was ready to pull her into his arms. But no such luck. Kelleigh straightened her stance, her face void of expression.

"I'll get Toru to send through our legal teams contact details. You can deal with them directly in the future. I want no part in your case."

He nodded once, turned and walked away.

As he jumped in his Landcruiser he glanced sideways to see a JLR ute parked next to his. It must belong to Kelleigh's team members. As his hands tightened around his steering wheel, a renewed determination flooded through him. It was finally good to see a definitive end to all his foolish emotions and attraction. He could refocus now. Gumtrees and his surrounding community was his priority and he'd do everything in his power to protect it. Whatever the cost.

Chapter 13

Paperwork littered every inch of Kelleigh's desk. She grumbled with every keystroke as she reviewed the surveying data collected over the past few days on her laptop. She rubbed at her eyes and tried to clear her head. She'd hardly slept a wink last night, lying awake, tossing and turning and watching the clock click slowly toward dawn. All she could think about was Troy. She'd done the unthinkable in slapping him and couldn't forget the hurt in his eyes when she said she never wanted to see him again.

She'd done it all to protect him. She had to keep him away from her so there would be no complications between them and no one got hurt.

When Troy had come up to her when Brian was venting his anger, she'd nearly thrown herself into his arms and burst into tears. She'd been terrified and all she wanted was for Troy to wrap his protective arms around her, hold her tight and get her out of there.

Spending time with Troy last night had changed her opinion of him yet again. He'd apologized for his outburst; she was impressed he was man enough to say sorry. He'd saved her from Brian's onslaught and seemed to know what she needed, offering to take her for a walk. The brief moment back in her room was torture. All she could think about was the night they'd spent together. She wanted to get out of there as quick as possible but her fingers kept fumbling as she tried to tie her wretched shoelaces. Because all she could think about in that moment was dragging him back into bed.

But that would have been wrong. Clarity came to her as she walked next to him though the gardens. She had two and a half weeks left to finish her feasibility studies and then she'd be going back to Melbourne. Troy would be doing everything to stop the development from being approved. All these elements, along with her bucketload of problems back home, were not a good combination. She would've loved another night with Troy, but there was one major issue that scared her more than anything. She doubted she'd be able to keep control of her heart. Falling for him was not an option.

Resting her elbows on the table, she hung her head and buried her face in the palms of her hands.

How was she ever going to live with what she did to him? She'd never hit anyone before. After living for years in fear of Rodrigo's short temper, she never thought she'd be the one to lash out. Looking at her hand, it was still red and stung. She hoped Troy was okay. She'd slapped him hard. Harder than she meant to or even thought was possible.

She wished she could change what had happened. Keeping up the façade that she was not affected by his presence was a constant struggle. Rambling on about work and her problems took her mind off wanting to feel every inch of his well-toned flesh. She'd thought babbling on about her issues would turn off any man. While her words may have been true, her actions certainly had not.

When he picked the rose, the prospect of security guards coming after them for vandalizing the grounds put her mind on track to ensure she kept her distance from Troy.

His kiss came out of nowhere and took her by surprise.

She wanted that kiss. Craved it. But knowing the stakes were against them, it took every ounce of her strength to stop. She couldn't let it go on any further. Letting her shock, anger and frustrations consume her, she had pushed him away, regardless of how much her body ached to have him. She couldn't afford to give in.

Then there was that slap. Where had that come from? She should've just pulled away, but no, she'd taken it too far. Now guilt ate away inside her.

She shook her head abruptly. What's done is done. There was nothing she could do about it. She had to stay clear of him, focus on getting her job done and leave this town as soon as possible.

Her email pinged with a new message. Thankful for the distraction, she scanned the screen as she opened the message from Toru; he wanted an update on how the council meeting went. *Asshole for leaving her to do it!* How was she going to describe the meeting from hell? Kelleigh rubbed at her temples as an ache started to form in her head. This never-ending stress; who needed it?

Reading the entire email, she grew more disgruntled with every line. He was coming back up on Friday to meet the environmental auditors with her and attend the gala dinner at the Hunter Valley Wine Trade Festival on Saturday night. That would be right. He only wants to come back here for the fancy festival, all at the company's expense. But if he wanted to hang out and schmooze industry representatives, suppliers, wholesalers and stockists—that was one task she'd gladly let him have.

A piercing beep burst from her laptop, making her jump. The red flashing banner alerted her to low battery life. She reached down beside her for her laptop bag to grab the power cable, and panic set in when it was not in the front pocket.

Throwing the bag on the ground, Kelleigh stood up and started to search her room. In her bedroom, under her jacket, through the pile of clothes, under the magazines and papers. The cable was nowhere to be found. Halfway across the living area she stopped in her stride and slapped her palm to her forehead.

Shit! I've left it at Gumtrees.

She'd been out on-site all day yesterday and had used Toru's presentation on USB at last night's presentation in the provided laptop. She hadn't needed to use her own computer since her meeting at Gumtrees. She must have forgotten to pack the cable in her haste to get away.

She wasn't one to believe in fate, the influence of the alignment of the planet and the stars, or unexplainable coincidences, but was this the universe giving her the opportunity to go and apologize to Troy?

She needed her power cord back and now had the chance to see Troy. Picking up the in-room phone, she called the kitchen to arrange her lunch-pack then finished dressing into her work gear, laced up her steel-caps and headed out the door.

As Kelleigh walked into the restaurant, she saw Grace restocking the fridge in behind the bar.

"Morning Grace," she called out as she walked over to the counter.

"Morning, lovey." Grace stood up and stretched her back. "How are you this morning? Brian was a bit of an ass to you last night, wasn't he?"

Kelleigh winced and nodded. His frightening, threatening face still lingered in her thoughts.

"Is my order ready yet?"

"Be about another five minutes or so. We've been busy this morning."

"Mind if I wait here?" Kelleigh asked as she took a seat.

"Not at all."

Kelleigh sat up, startled when Grace approached her, looked at her through narrowed eyes and leaned on the counter in front of her. "I saw you leave with Troy again last night. Anything happen I should know about?" Her look was serious, curious, one of interest, but not menacing in any way.

Kelleigh blinked. Did Grace already know that she'd slapped him in the face? "Last night ... we just went for a walk over in the gardens."

"Anything else happen? I've seen the way you look at him." She grinned, with the spark of knowledge in her eyes. "I'm no fool. It's been there since the first night you lured him to your room."

Kelleigh's eyes widen in shock. "If I recall correctly, it was pretty even on getting each other in to bed. We were both consenting. And for your information ... no, nothing else happened last night." Other than she hit him and felt terrible about it.

Grace's expression softened and a wide smile broadened across her face. "I'm just teasing you, lovey. Troy's like my own son, especially since his mum was my best friend before she passed away. I know he's a grown man and can do what he pleases, but I still like to look out for him. He doesn't need his heart broken again, so don't go messing with it if you're only here for a few weeks."

Kelleigh slipped her hands into her lap. Everywhere she went people wanted to tell her what to do. There'd been Rodrigo, her boss and now Grace wanted to meddle with her non-existent love life. "It was one night. He was willing and so was I. It won't happen again, I assure you." Her actions last night would definitely see to that.

"Pity a gorgeous gal like you doesn't plan on staying around. While we love the tourists, the travelers and the seasonal workers, they all keep passing on through. We have such a beautiful region, full of possibilities. You just need to know where to look."

Stay in the Hunter Valley? As if that would ever happen. It certainly wasn't for her. She had her sister, Fran, back at home whose baby was due soon and her friends—although she questioned their true status since Rodrigo had skipped town. No, Melbourne was her home and always would be. In a place like this there were too many limitations for someone like her who worked in engineering and projects. The pay wouldn't be as good for a start and there's no way she wanted to work up in the mining districts. So even considering the idea for a fleeting second was ludicrous. And besides, she'd miss Franny way too much.

"Thanks, but I'll be heading home in a couple of weeks so you have no need to be concerned about Troy. I have no intention of seeing him again. Well ... after this morning. I've left my laptop's power cord out at their office and I need to go and pick it up on my way out to Larry's."

Grace nodded, looking satisfied, yet disappointed at the same time. Kelleigh turned as the kitchen door swung open and a woman dressed in a white chef's coat walked out with her lunch-pack, and slid it across the counter to her with a broad smile. "Say hello to Larry for us. We miss him coming into the pub. We all hope he gets better soon."

"Thanks. I'll be sure to give him the message." Kelleigh nodded, grabbed her food and headed out to her car.

The stifling humid air struck Kelleigh when she walked out of the cool air conditioning. She yanked open the Landcruiser's door, climbed inside and placed the food on the seat beside her. Away from Grace, she could breathe easily and didn't feel like every move she made was being scrutinized. This trip was supposed to give her a break from all her problems, but somehow she seemed to be creating more for herself.

She peered out of the windscreen up to the threatening gray skies. Storm clouds loomed over the crest of the Brokenback Mountains heading toward the Valley. *Great!* This was not what she needed. Rain caused delays and she didn't want to have to spend one more day in this place than necessary. She rolled her shoulders, trying to dislodge the knots and tension that had built up. Cranking the key in the engine, she ripped the vehicle into gear. With no more delays, it was time to visit Gumtrees.

Chapter 14

"Are you going to tell me how you got that beauty of a red mark on your face, or do I have to guess?" Nick asked as he placed another case of wine on the pallet he was loading with Troy.

"You don't want to know, mate." Troy said, grabbing another box from the back of the cellar and placing it on top of the pile of wine they were getting ready to take to the trade show in two days' time. Spending all morning responding to his lawyer's emails, sifting through reports and looking for something, anything, to stop the JLR development had managed to keep him busy. Now getting ready for the show was also helping to keep his mind off last night with Kelleigh and the pain still lingering in his left cheek.

"Wouldn't happen to involve a certain chick, would it? Kelleigh, by any chance? What on earth did you do to deserve that?"

Troy smirked, Nick was too observant. "It was a simple misunderstanding. I apologized to her for getting upset at our meeting, nearly threw Brian out of the pub because he was being an ass toward her and then afterwards, we went for a walk in the gardens. I thought things were going well. Then … I tried to kiss her. Of course, it didn't quite go as planned."

Nick burst out laughing. "Oh you poor bugger."

"In some ways it worked wonders. It knocked the sense back into me. Remind me never to get involved with a woman with issues." He added up the quantity of cartons of each type of wine and wrote them down on to his stock consignment sheet.

"Everyone's got issues; except me of course." Nick smiled cheekily as they headed out through the storage cellar's sliding door and locked it securely behind them. "I wouldn't give up on women just yet; she obviously wasn't the right one."

Troy sighed as they walked back through the production area to the work office at the front of the shed.

"Well, I'm not going out of my way to find her if she exists. She'll have to come and find me."

Nick shook his head as Troy walked behind him into the office and sat down in front of his laptop. Nick took the seat in front of the computer. Glancing over the stock sheet, Troy recalculated his totals and, once satisfied, handed the sheet to Nick. "Here. All done. Do you want to enter this consignment, or shall I?"

"I'll do it," Nick took the paper from his hand. "You get onto all that legal stuff. We've got two weeks until JLR submit their application to council. We have to find a way to stop it before then. Has Max come up with anything yet?"

"She's going to join us at the council's open meeting when JLR submit their application. That's when we can present any information we have against the development."

"Excellent. When's that so I can put it in my calendar?"

"It's in two weeks on Wednesday at 10.30 a.m."

"Done."

Troy returned his attention to the emailed information from Maxine. Opening up an attachment, he clicked the button to print off the document. JLR had months of preparation in their favor. Deep down, Troy knew a company like this would not be doing on-site studies if they didn't think their development application was going to be successful. Was this an uphill battle that he couldn't win? Frustrated, he jumped out of the chair, walked over to the printer and waited for the thirty-page document to print. He had to find a way to stop Larry's place being turned into a golf course.

As Nick typed away at the computer, Troy started to scan the first page of the printout. All the legal jargon was enough to make his brain hurt from information overload. He rubbed at his temple with his fingertips, then brushed down the side of his face to his swollen cheek. Kelleigh had certainly left her mark on him, unfortunately not just on his skin.

A knock on the door made him jolt.

There she stood, but why?

"Kelleigh? What are you doing here?" he said through a strained jaw. After everything she said and did last night, how did she have the nerve to show her face here?

"Miss Johnstone." Nick greeted her politely, before turning around on the chair and grinning up at him. "Looks like someone's found you."

Troy glared back at Nick, far from happy at his joke.

"Um ..." Kelleigh paused. "I must have left my laptop cord in your office the other day and came to pick it up. There was no one in reception so when I saw the Landcruiser over here, I thought it best to come over. And ... I'd like to talk to you please, Troy."

Damn, she looked hot in hi-vis work gear and a pair of steel-caps. With her hair pulled back into some kind of braid, it exposed the soft skin of her neck. Where he'd kissed her. Tasted her skin. Breathed in her essence. *No, damn it.* He clenched his hand and dug his fingernails into his palms so he could control his thoughts. "About what?" he leaned back against the wall, folded his arms and crossed his ankles.

Her eyes darted to Nick and then back to him. "Any chance we can talk … in private?"

"Well, look at the time." Nick slapped his hand down on the desk, pushed back from his chair and started for the door. "That storm's going to hit soon and I need to get back over to the main office to help Maria."

"Nick." Troy stood his ground. "You don't have to leave. Kelleigh won't be staying long." He remained glaring at Kelleigh. She could have easily walked into the restaurant where one of the staff would have assisted her to the office to get her cable. Why on earth did she come all the way over here to the sheds when she told him she never wanted to see him again?

"Nah, mate, I'll leave you to it. We have guests arriving soon and I need to make sure the cabins are ready." He waved goodbye as he shuffled out the doorway past Kelleigh and disappeared outside as the first raindrops started to fall loudly on the tin roof of the shed.

"You said you wanted to talk, so talk." He closed his eyes momentarily and tried to think of something else, anything else, other than the scent of her perfume that filled the air as she stepped inside the office.

With a few cautious steps she came closer, hooked her finger under his chin and turned his face to the side so she could see the shiny mark emblazoned on his skin.

"Does it hurt?" she winced.

"Not really." As if he'd ever admit to her, it hurt like absolute hell. "And you said you wouldn't hurt a fly." He pulled his chin free from her hold.

"I came to apologize. I've never hit anyone before and feel terrible about it. You took me by surprise when you kissed me and I reacted in every conceivable wrong way." His breath hitched and his skin tingled when she placed her soft hand on his forearm. This was not good; she was standing too close to him. "You have to believe me when I say I truly am sorry."

The desperate plea in her voice would have been convincing enough for her to get pardon from death row. He had to look away, opting for the view of the rain outside the window.

The air around him filled with warmth as she leaned in toward him. Before he could turn, her lips pressed ever so gently against his swollen cheek. Lingering for what seemed like an eternity on his skin.

When she stepped back, he looked at her. Confusion swirled through his mind. "What was that for?"

"Part of my apology. Last night was all a mess and my actions were uncalled for."

He dropped his arms down to his sides. "I'll be fine."

She didn't look convinced.

"I never anticipated meeting someone like you and never expected the odds to stack against us. The night we spent together was the most amazing time I've ever had in my life, but my work has put us in opposition. My past hangs over my head. My time here is only temporary. In consideration of all these factors, I thought it best to stay away from you. I didn't want to lead you on, didn't want to get hurt and didn't want to like you as much as I do. My frustrations got the better of me last night, but that's no excuse for hitting you. I mean it when I say I'm sorry."

What was that? She liked him?

"I couldn't bear the thought of leaving and you thinking I hated you. Because that's not the case. Not at all."

She stepped closer, her eyes penetrating deeply into his. Unable to look away, his mouth ran dry, making it hard to swallow. She reached out toward him and started to snake her hands around his waist, but he grabbed her wrists in time and stopped her advances. "What are you doing?" Lord, give him strength.

She tried to nudge closer, but he held her at bay. "I want to show you how sorry I am."

His mind swirled. What was she doing to him? What was he supposed to do when he could feel his resolve starting to crack?

She edged her way out of his hold, rested her hands on to his chest and inched her lips toward his. He closed his eyes and tried to make sense out of all this. Feeling her breath on his face had an inexplicable effect on him, causing his pulse to rise along with his want. When he opened his eyes, he couldn't fight it any more. Grasping the back of her neck, he drew her in to him and slammed his lips against hers. Her tongue shot into his mouth and he tasted it with hunger. His lips seared against hers as he gasped for each breath of air.

Fuck!

His ears pricked up when he heard one of the work vehicles pull into the shed. He released his clasp on Kelleigh and stepped away from her as Jimmy, his field assistant and laborer, ducked his head around the doorway.

"Hey boss. Oh shit! Sorry to interrupt."

Troy rubbed at his arm, not knowing where to look. "No, you're fine." Riddled with guilt and unable to hide the color he felt flaring in his cheeks. "What's up?"

"I've got to head into town to the doctors. Think I might need some stiches in my hand. Cut it open on my secateurs." He waved his wrapped-up hand.

"Wait up a sec and I'll drive you?"

"Nah. I'll be okay. You look kind of busy." He waved as he walked out the door.

Troy hesitated, torn between doing his duty as a boss and want for Kelleigh. "I need to make sure he's okay." Kelleigh nodded, still looking flustered from their kiss. But before Troy could make it out into the shed, Jimmy sped off in the car. *Damn it!*

As Jimmy disappeared down the driveway, the heavens opened up even more and torrential rain pelted down onto the ground. The sound of the heavy downpour on the tin roof was near deafening.

He turned back to see Kelleigh standing awkwardly in the middle of the room.

Placing his hands on his hips, he pondered on what to do. His dick was semi-hard. His body ached. His mind full of Kelleigh and that kiss. What could he do in the rain, in the middle of the wine production shed while it was bucketing down rain? Nothing. Then he smiled as an idea brewed inside his head.

"Guess you won't be working out on-site in this weather?"

She shook her head.

"Got any other plans?"

She shook her head again.

"Good."

He walked over to the desk, picked up his security card, grabbed Kelleigh by the hand and led her toward the back of the shed.

Chapter 15

"Where are we going?" Kelleigh asked as Troy guided her past all the production equipment—conveyers, vats, steel bins and other contraptions. All she wanted to do was lock the office door and continue where they left off.

"I thought you might like a tour," Troy said, coming to a halt in front of a large sliding door at the back of the shed.

"A tour?" If it involved his naked body, yep, she was in. "A tour of what?"

Taking out his security card from his shirt pocket, he swiped it through the scanner and the door released with a loud click.

"Why do you need security out here for?"

"This." He slid the huge door open wide enough for them to walk through.

"Wow!" Kelleigh gasped as she stepped through into the huge cellar. Three long rows of wine barrels, racked up to the ceiling, stretched out before her.

"We had to install security because there was too much theft going on. Guests, seasonal harvest pickers, local kids thinking it's fun stealing—who knows." Troy flicked a switch that threw a soft ambient light throughout the cellar and a shimmered golden off the oak barrels before he closed the door behind them.

She looked around in awe. This was definitely taking her focus off what happened back in the office. Was that his plan? He needed a distraction too? Had she overstepped the boundaries and blurred the lines of their relationship, when no such thing could ever exist?

"It stinks in here." Kelleigh said, wrinkling her nose at the musty smell in the air.

"Really? I must have grown accustomed to it, I don't smell a thing." Crow's-feet etched at the corner of his eyes as he smiled. "Watch your step around this pallet." He held out his hand to help her. "This is all the wine for the festival tomorrow."

"That's a lot of wine." She eyed the stack of cases. "Are you going?"

"Yeah, Jessica's roped me into doing a session tomorrow afternoon on vineyard management."

"Who's Jessica?"

"Um ..." She didn't think that was such a difficult question. "She's the event organizer."

Hmm. She detected there was more to Jessica, but didn't pursue the subject. Being alone with Troy was all she could think about at present. She ran her fingers over the edges of the oak barrels, feeling their smooth texture beneath her fingertips as she followed him along one of the aisles.

"The left side is our shiraz, the right side is our verdelho and chardonnay and the middle row is my favorite—our semillon." Pride was evident on his face as he patted the belly of a barrel. "Here, this is what I wanted to show you." He stopped at a cleared area halfway down the cellar where four bar stools sat next to a table. On its surface sat a box of glasses, several bottles of wine and few weird-looking utensils.

"What's all this for?" She picked up a bottle from the table and admired the Gumtrees Vineyard label—a tall eucalypt tree emblazoned in bronze with the words either side of its trunk. An elegant yet simple logo.

"If you're up for it, I thought I'd give you a personal wine tasting."

"Oh!" She placed the bottle back down. Him. Alone in a cellar. Alcohol. What a tempting combination. All this was great, but he hadn't said anything about their kiss and it was sending her mental, not knowing what he was thinking. Was that it? Just a kiss and time to move on? No one could kiss like that and not be affected by it. "That sounds nice, but are we going to talk about what happened back there in the office?"

He reached for her hand, drew her hard up against the plane of his chest and whispered in her ear. "Oh, I have every intention of continuing our office discussion." She closed her eyes. His deep voice, with a promise of so much more, resonated throughout her entire body. His warm breath shot down the side of her neck, giving her goosebumps all over. His lips lingering beside her ear made her head dizzy. All of this before touching a drop of wine.

Placing his hands on her arms, he guided her backward and helped her to sit up on one of the bar stools beside the table. She shuffled around, side to side on the seat, to find a comfortable position.

He placed his hands down, one on either side of her hips; seriousness drew across his face as he leaned before her. "You have caused me a great deal of grief since I met you. You've threatened me with a tire wrench, threatened to buy my home, threatened to leave me alone. Yet here you are again today with another story. I'm usually an easygoing type of bloke, but with you, I never know what to believe. You certainly know how to confuse a man. One minute I never want to see you again, the next I want to get you back into bed. Shall we work out what I should do with you while tasting a few samples of wine? Are you up for a little game?"

"What kind of game?" Her stomach fluttered, her mouth ran dry.

"A wine-tasting game. Correct answers will earn you a point toward taking you to bed. Get something wrong; that'll be a point toward sending you home. First to five wins."

"But I've never done a wine tasting before. I know nothing about wine so I don't think that's very fair. How about something easy? How about if I just like the taste or not?"

"I'll be able to tell that by your reaction. After everything that's happened, this mark on my face, what you said before in the office—I need a little more convincing about which outcome to take." He inched closer to her. His gaze lingered on her lips before he looked into her eyes. "You're going to have to trust me. For what I have in mind, I think you might enjoy it."

Her lips parted, rendering her speechless as Troy's eyes hinted at mischief. How could she refuse? Before she could ask any more questions, he pressed his lips to hers, taking the air from her lungs as he did so. Exploring her top lip, then her bottom lip; all sending shivers up her spine.

He stopped and the smile reached his eyes. "So what do you say?"

She would happily taste anything he put in her mouth right now. Skipping the wine tasting all together sounded like a better option, but she was intrigued. Here she was alone with him in this beautiful cellar. Work cancelled because of the teaming rain. Nowhere to go. Nothing to do. Temptation standing before her. Uncertainty flickered through her mind, but curiosity got the better of her. Sure, she would play this game. "I'm up for a little adventure." She nodded. "Does that kiss count as a point towards going to bed?"

He shook his finger playfully in front of her as he took a step back to the table. She observed his every move as he prepared and poured two small glasses of wine.

"We haven't started yet. First, you need to know there are four main areas to taste a wine: sight, nose, palate and finish. I'll talk you through each step and keep it simple. See how you go. This first one is a sauvignon blanc." He handed her the glass. "First, swirl the glass around gently observing the color, then inhale its aroma, followed by taking a sip."

Holding the stem of the glass, she did as he instructed and took her first sip, before drinking down the remaining contents in one large gulp.

His eyes widened as she licked her lips. "Sorry, wasn't I supposed to do that?"

He shook his head, a broad grin touching his lips. "Strike one. That's a point toward sending you on your way."

She gasped. Was he serious? "Well then, better pour the next one," she said, screwing up her nose as the aftertaste of the wine hit her. "Because I didn't like that one at all. It's too light and fruity." As she placed her empty glass on the table, he stepped toward her. His hands cupped the side of her face and he leaned in to kiss her. Opening her mouth, she breathed him in as he flicked his tongue, laced with the sweet taste of wine, against hers. His fingertips glided across her skin, traveled down the side of her neck, across her shirt, and opened the top two buttons of her shirt. Her heart rate pumped faster as he slowly exposed her flesh. A gentle moan deep within his throat shuddered through her before he retreated back a couple of steps.

She licked her lips, savoring the taste of him. "I think I just changed my mind. I do like the aftertaste of that one after all."

His sapphire blue eyes blazed. "I think that is a point toward bed."

Oh, this was getting interesting.

"That makes the score even, so you better bring on the next one."

The second tasting of a verdehlo was just as bad, or good, if you take in the kiss and the fact that her shirt was now completely undone. Another point toward bed.

"What did you think of that one?" Troy asked about the third wine, yet another verdelho.

"Hmm. Let me see." She grabbed the bottle and read the wine label on the back. "A sweet, fresh flavorsome wine with a well-balanced fruity palate."

"Hey," he grabbed the bottle from her hands and placed it on the table. "We can't have you cheating. That's not allowed." He glanced at her and pondered for a moment before he opened a small drawer underneath the table and drew out a black satin sash. Kelleigh gulped at the sight of the silky tie as he smoothed it through his hands. "This is an old Award ribbon we no longer have on display. To avoid any more of your tricks and so you can truly appreciate the wine, I'd like to cover your eyes. Is that okay?" The desire burning in his eyes sent a wave of heat straight between her legs. She'd never been blindfolded before. This was unchartered territory. She liked looking at Troy, seeing his reaction, knowing what he was doing and where he was. But blindfolded? He held up the ribbon before her. "All you have to do is follow the sound of my voice and enjoy the wine. Taking away one of your senses will enhance your sense of smell, taste, and hearing. Okay?"

With her heart thudding in her chest, she fell under the hypnotic resonance in his voice. She nodded slowly as he lowered the sash over her eyes and secured it firmly.

"You can remove it at any time. I won't tie it on tight."

Her fingers trembled as she touched the satin covering her

eyes. She couldn't see a thing. It was pitch black.

When she stopped fidgeting around making the tie comfortable, she took a deep breath to calm her nerves. The sound of the rain hammered on the roof up above, but now she noticed so much more. She could hear the soft steps Troy took in the direction of the table. The clinking of glasses. The metal cap being unscrewed off the top of a bottle. The glug, glug, glug of the liquid being poured. And more than anything she could sense Troy's every move.

"This forth wine is a chardonnay. Citrusy, unwooded. Ready to drink." Troy took her hand and wrapped her fingers around the glass. Trying not to giggle, she attempted to swirl, sniff and sip the wine like he showed her to do before. The scent tickled her nostrils and as the liquid hit her taste buds, the flavor exploded like skittles inside her mouth. With a mouthful of wine, she coughed, spluttered and dribbled the wine down her front, wetting her skin, her bra and her shirt in the process. She fumbled but managed to place the glass on the table and started to wipe up the mess with her shirtsleeve.

"Tut, tut, tut," Troy tisked, his voice light, playful and full of sexy as she felt him come near. His body filling her personal space with an alluring warmth. "I don't like to see all my hard work and wine wasted, so that's definitely a point for sending you home." His fingertip wiped away a droplet of wine from her chin before following a trail down along her throat. "Such a waste."

He edged her legs wider apart and his lips found their way to the side of her neck. Tilting her head, his tongue licked along the length of her throat and kissed away the dash of wine she had spilt before he returned to her mouth. Her breath hitched as the explosion of flavor—spice, citrus and sweetness—fused together as their mouths connected. Boldly, his fingertips started exploring, grazing over the wet fabric of her bra. Drawing along the edge of material, he slipped them underneath and found her hardened nipple. He deepened his kiss and breaths became heavier as he fondled her breast. Leaning against the back of the bar stool, she arched her chest into his touch and entangled her hands through his hair, the soft strands sliding through her fingertips. Her eyes fluttered shut behind the blindfold when he bobbed his head down, pulled the fabric of her bra aside and took her nipple into his mouth. Her pulse thudded in her ears as he licked and sucked her with his warm, wet tongue. Flicked and circled around her aroused bud. Creeping her hands down over his shoulders and onto his back, she tugged at his polo shirt, pulling it free from his jeans and tried to pull it over his head.

But he stopped her, realigned her bra, drew back and left her sitting there gasping for air.

She could hear him licking his lips, and pictured him looking rather pleased with himself for leaving her in a state of disarray. What was he doing? Why did he stop? Where was that bottle of wine? She wanted to grab it and pour it all over herself if he was going to do that to her again. She wanted him. Enough of this teasing. Was this some kind of torturous payback for her slapping him? She never had experienced much foreplay before. Rodrigo was too self-centered. But this game with Troy had her aching and craving for satisfaction. She wriggled on her seat, straightened her shirt up and ensured the blindfold was in place. With several calming breaths she regained her composure, but the fire within her was well lit and she didn't know how much more of this she could take.

"I think that deserves a point for bed. Don't you think?" How could he sound so casual after that?

She sensed him grinning as he poured the next set of glasses. "Are you enjoying the wine tasting?"

"I've never been to one before so I've got no comparison. If they're all like this, I must make the effort to go to them more often. So far it's been … interesting. How am I doing?"

"You're doing just fine, trust me." He placed the next glass in her hand. "This wine is Gumtree's prize semillon."

She lifted the glass up to her nose and sniffed before she touched the rim to her lips and took a small sip. "You're enjoying this, aren't you?"

They finished the wine and placed the glasses down on the table. She spread her legs wider, allowing him to nudge up close to her again. Tingles danced across her skin as he glided his hands up along her arms, toying with the top of her open shirt before peeling it off her shoulders.

"I have wine and a beautiful woman here, what's not to enjoy?" His breath, all hot and heavy in her ear as he freed her from her top. His mouth claimed hers as she wrapped her arms around him and ran her hands over his strong muscles.

"I think I need a couple more points for the result I want." She whispered over their kisses. "What do I need to do to get them?" Slowly she glided her fingers, over the soft cotton of his shirt hanging loosely around his hips, to the front of his jeans. Finding the edge of his leather belt, she undid it and popped open the top button of his jeans. Troy tensed, breath full of fire on her neck as she carefully unzipped his pants and rubbed her hand up the length of his hard erection bulging within his trunks.

"I think you may have managed to gain another one." He murmured as he pushed against her hand.

"What do I need to do for the last point?"

She smiled as Troy unfastened her belt, undid her workpants and teased her as he stroked across the front of her cotton panties. She gasped when his firm hands grabbed her around the hips and drew her off the bar stool. With her blindfold still secure, he guided her toward the sidewall where she recalled seeing a single barrel lying at the end of one of the racks. Standing behind her, he shimmied his hand down inside her panties and explored between her legs. She was so wet. Her whole body quivered as his fingers probed into her.

"I think you've easily reached five points. There's a barrel in front of you. Bend." He whispered into her ear, nudged her forward and guided her hands on to the wine barrel. *Oh my ...* His warm hands circled down over her bare back, across her hips, over the curve of her buttocks, and pulled her trousers down along with her panties. Fingers trailed back up between her legs, feeding the fire within.

She was about to protest when he stopped touching her, but the soft rustle of fabric behind her, the flip of a wallet opening, the tearing of plastic and the snap of a condom being rolled on, promised so much more. Then he pressed his erection between her legs, guided the head toward her opening and slowly eased inside her. *Fuck!* She threw her head back and groaned in delight as he buried himself inside her. With one hand, she reached back and clung on to his thigh, feeling every one of his muscles strain beneath his denim jeans as he slowly withdrew and penetrated her again.

"God, you feel so good." He delved deep inside her again. She closed her eyes and rocked back against his hard body as one of his hands sought out and cupped her breast. Squeezing it and tweaking her nipple, he thrust slowly into her again, making her knees buckle. "Is this okay?" His voice sounded strained, as if struggling for control.

Her mind rattled. His dick was inside her. Blood was surging through her veins like a bushfire in the Blue Mountains. Every time he slid in and out, she panted to catch her breath.

"Yes, but touch me." She took his hand from her breast and guided it down between her legs. He needed no further direction as he slipped his finger between her folds of skin and rubbed her swollen bud. As he circled and rubbed her arousal she bit down hard on her lip, to stop from screaming out loud.

Air rushed in and out of her lungs in short sharp bursts as her hips rocked back and forth. Carefully he pulled back again, before burying the full length of his shaft hard into her again.

Damn, that felt so good.

Driving into her sent shockwaves up her spine and tingles pooling at the base of her neck. Clenching around him, she begged him to go deeper. He thrust harder and harder. Giving her everything she could take. Her fingernails clawed at the wooden surface of the barrel. Her toes curled inside her steel cap boots. Her ears hummed with the sound of her pulse as Troy penetrated her with his rock-hard cock.

A loud clap of thunder shattered through the skies outside and she came. Quaking under his touch, she felt his own release. He shuddered and wrapped his arms around her belly. Holding her close, he regained his breath before he withdrew. When she stood up, she finally removed the blindfold and he buried his face into her neck. Reaching up, she touched his cheek and inhaled his spicy scent.

"Do you do this on all of your private wine tasting tours?" she teased, allowing her heart rate to settle.

"I might have to start offering this as an optional extra," he chuckled, kissing her cheek.

"I'll never be able to drink another glass of semillon ever again without thinking about this." She blushed as they both shuffled to do up their pants. He picked up and handed her shirt for her to redress before he tucked his own back into place.

He grinned as he drew her into his arms and kissed her softly on the lips. "I never knew personal wine tastings tours could be so much fun. I'll never be able to do a wine tour in here again without thinking about this."

Kelleigh closed her eyes and took a step out of his arms.

"You okay?" he reached out and caught her arm.

"Um ... yeah. We got a bit carried away, didn't we?" She covered her flushed cheeks with her hands. "I really only came out here to apologize and get my computer cable." She lowered her eyes to the ground. "Unfortunately, this doesn't change anything. I still have a job to do and will be heading home in two weeks."

"Don't be so worried. I'm fully aware of our situation. I'll be okay, how about you?"

She nodded. He might be okay, but would she? Her whole body buzzed after that orgasm and somehow she had to find the strength to walk away and never see him again.

"Think of this as I accept your apology wholeheartedly." He grinned cheekily, tugged on the front of her shirt and kissed her softly on the cheek. "Come on, it sounds like the rain has eased up." Troy returned to the table and started to clean up. He screwed the lids back onto the opened wine bottles and loaded all the used wine glasses into a basket. "We need to stop off here quickly in the office before we go and get your cable," he said as he started to lead her back to the entrance. "There's one thing I forgot about."

"Yeah. What's that?"

"It's nothing to worry about because Nick, Maria and I are the only ones with access, but I need to log on to the computer and delete the last thirty minutes or so of security footage. I forgot about the cameras."

Chapter 16

Kelleigh opened the curtains on Friday morning to heavy, overcast skies, but nothing could dampen her mood after making up with Troy yesterday afternoon. After her apology and the steamy sex, she was looking forward to a day working out on-site with her team.

Walking into the dining area dressed in her hi-vis gear, she found her JLR crew finishing off large plates of bacon and eggs. Duncan, her geo-technician, flicked his thick brown curls, smiled with a mouthful of food and slopped up egg on his plate with a slice of toast. Lucas, her operations tech, hunched his slim shoulders forward and slurped on his cup of tea. Roger, her all-round laborer, shoveled cereal into his mouth while Paul, her surveyor, with his blond dreads tied back into a ponytail, looked like he'd just rolled out of bed and rubbed his tired eyes.

"Morning all," she waved to them as she walked over to the buffet breakfast. The aroma of sweet bacon, greasy eggs and fresh toast made her mouth water. It all smelled so good. After yesterday with Troy, she'd certainly worked up an appetite. She grabbed a warm plate and loaded it up with food and licked her lips at the sight of all the pastries and croissants lined up next to the condiments and toast. She hesitated as images of her ex glaring at her flooded her mind. He would've condemned her for eating such delicacies. Walking along the buffet, her steps were lighter knowing he was no longer breathing down her neck telling her to watch her waistline. She was going to devour whatever she wanted. She grabbed two chocolate-filled treats and placed them onto her already loaded plate and was going to enjoy every last crumb.

She returned to the table and started to hook into her breakfast.

"We've got a busy day ahead of us, boys, while it's not raining," she said. "With it being so wet, I'm not sure how far we'll get the drilling truck down into the paddock without it getting bogged. Let's pray for sunshine so we can finish this job and go home."

"Hell yeah," the others all said together.

"Toru is coming up again today to meet with me and the flora and fauna auditor. We've never used this mob before so I'll see if they need anything from us while you guys continue with the drilling."

"It's going to be a muddy day out in those paddocks," Duncan's eyes sparkled as he rubbed his hands together. "You ready to get down and dirty with us again, Kel?"

She nodded and nibbled on her pastry. "I wouldn't have it any other way. Beats the hell out of being in the office, doesn't it?"

Lucas stood up, scraping his chair loudly on the wooden floor. "I'm done. I need to make a phone call so I'll meet you outside in about fifteen minutes." He pushed his chair back in under the table and left the room without another word.

"Is Lucas all right?" Kelleigh asked her team.

"He's fine. Just moody as always. I think I can speak for

everyone," Duncan said, "but thank God you scored the role as project leader on this gig rather than him. I wouldn't have come on this trip if he was our supervisor."

Kelleigh stopped mid-chew. Duncan's comment was one of the nicest things she'd heard from him regarding her efforts at work. She may feel out of her depth at times, but this bunch of guys offered great support. They were like brothers to her. All the men nodded in agreement, taking their last mouthfuls of breakfast and leaving clean plates; not even a crumb or smear of ketchup in sight.

"Thanks, guys." She hoped she wouldn't let them down.

"We'll see you out on-site soon." Paul said, stretching his arms up over his head and standing up from the table.

"No worries. I won't be far behind you."

Kelleigh watched the three men leave the room and the peace and quiet settled around her. As always, her thoughts returned to Troy when she was left alone.

"What's got you all goofy-eyed and in such a good mood this morning?"

Kelleigh jumped in her seat as Grace walked up to the table to clear the dishes away.

"Nothing." Kelleigh's cheeks flushed.

"Oh sweetie. I've been working in a pub for years. I've seen it all. You, my dear, look like you've had one hell of a good time with a fella. Care to tell me I'm wrong?"

Kelleigh's mouth gaped open.

Grace put the pile of plates back down on the table, wiped her hands on her apron. "May I?" she asked, pointing to the chair.

Kelleigh nodded. Grace pulled out one of the chairs and sat across from her with a glint shimmering brightly in her eye. "Now ... which one of those boys of yours has done this to you?"

"Oh Grace, what am I going to do?" She leaned forward on

the table and covered her face with her hands.

"Causing problems in your team, are you? I see that tall one with the dreads, what's his name, Paul, staring at you every now and then. Is it him?"

Kelleigh sat up and looked at Grace in confusion. "Paul? No. It's not anyone in my team." She sighed, placing her palms down on the table. "Do I really have to tell you who it is? You seem to know everything going on around here."

"Oh no. Not Troy. What were you thinking?"

"It just happened. He's in front of me every time I turn around. He's rescued me twice. The first time from my broken-down car, the second time from Brian's fury. Then, yesterday afternoon when I stopped by to get my power cord, he provided shelter for me when the storm hit. Being alone with him while Mother Nature unleashed that downpour was ... let's just say ... intense."

Grace shook her head, her eyes full of disappointment. "Of all the men in this community you could have a fling with, you had to pick him?"

"Why are you so protective of him? Can't he make his own decisions?" Grace sounded like an overbearing mother.

"Because he's a good man, just like his mother, God rest her soul. He deserves only the best after all he's been through."

Kelleigh peered at Grace, her interest piqued. "And what exactly has he been through?"

Grace hesitated. Had she said too much? Her eyes darted around her to see if anyone was close by. "He lost his mother and his wife in tragic circumstances, both have affected him deeply. That's all I'll say on the matter."

Kelleigh tapped her fingertips on top of the table. So there was more to Troy than she first suspected. There was some other reason why he remained single, she was sure of it. But it didn't matter; she was out of there in a couple of weeks. Regardless of his personal situation, he'd helped her in some small way. She now felt good about herself again and her confidence was coming back. She'd been numb for way too long.

She cocked her head. "Grace, do you believe in fate? Maybe there is a reason why we met. Maybe we needed each other at this point in our lives. To help each other out, even if it is for a short period of time."

Grace's eyes clouded with sadness. "You're the first woman to capture Troy's eye in quite some time. That's saying something. It's not only Troy I look out for; it's everyone, because in this community, we're all like family. But Troy is extra special to me."

Kelleigh thought about her own family. Franny, on the northern edge of the city, struggling every day, all for love. Her parents living hours away from Melbourne in Bendigo. Her father controlling. Her mother too timid. She shuddered at the reminder of how close she'd come to being like them with Rodrigo. "That's what I love about this place. You all look out for each other. In Melbourne, I didn't even know my neighbors in the apartment next door to me."

Sadness washed over Grace's eyes. "I don't know how you live like that."

Kelleigh hated it too. Other than Franny, she started to wonder how many true friends she had. Not one offered to help her when she was in dire trouble. They were all fake and a façade, just like her relationship with Rodrigo. Suddenly the thought of going back to Melbourne made her chest feel empty.

Oh well, she had two weeks left here in the Hunter Valley so she better make the most of it.

She pushed back her chair and slapped her hands down onto her thighs. "I've got to get going out to the site."

"I can't believe Larry's ol' farm is going to become a golf course. It doesn't seem right to me. It's prime farmland going to waste. But in my business, I can't knock the potential tourism your new golf course is going to bring to the area, and I know the Japanese love a good drink." Grace stood up and collected the dirty dishes off the table. "And as for you and Troy, you've had some fun, but that's enough."

Thanks for one last reminder, Grace. But she was right; there would be no more Troy.

Grace had successfully altered Kelleigh's mood, making her drag her feet on the way back to her room to collect her things for the day. This place and the people in it had started to weave its way into her heart in such a short span of time. There was something magical about the sense of community, the countryside, the energy in the air ... and Troy. It was going to make it hard to say farewell and return to her life in Melbourne.

***

After wading through thick mud and knee-high wet grass out in Larry's paddocks, Kelleigh, Toru and the environmental auditor, Jerry, stood on the back veranda of Larry's house and looked over the detailed maps on which she'd marked out all the points where her team had to drill for soil samples. It had taken her ages, but she needed to ensure they collected enough data so she'd be able to calculate the correct foundations for construction.

"Jerry," Toru rubbed at one of his thick black eyebrows, "you know we only need a brief report for the development application. From our research, there is nothing of concern in this area that will prevent our development from proceeding. Right?" Toru asked.

"Look, these original vegetation maps are really old." Jerry pulled out another map from underneath Kelleigh's pile. "This access on to the land has given us a good chance to do a thorough flora and fauna audit. I've found a few endangered red gums as we walked around, but with correct mitigation there should be no cause for concern."

"Good. I'm sure you won't find anything else, we've done checks already." Toru sweated profusely and continually wiped his brow with a handkerchief drawn from his pocket.

"I'm sure you'll get a good report, Toru." Jerry winked at him.

Kelleigh shot glances back and forth between the two men. What was that?

"Better get to work. See you later on." Jerry waved as he walked across the veranda with heavy footsteps, and took off down the paddock in his vehicle. Feigning a smile, Kelleigh shuddered, trying to ignore the sensation of spiders crawling up her back now she was left standing alone with Toru. Something was not right.

She grabbed her map and drew Toru's attention to it again. "After looking at the new designs, I've reworked the layout and position for the new villas and added in extra sampling sections up here on the main foothill."

Toru's eyes squinted as she pointed to an area of concentrated red marks on the map. "That is not necessary. No extras are required. Take the minimum samples you need and send them to Jerry in Maitland for testing." Toru didn't even look at the map.

"Jerry? I thought he was only doing the flora and fauna assessment, not our soil and water analysis. I've arranged to use our regular testing facilities in Melbourne?"

"Too far to send. Jerry's company does everything and will be able to perform all the necessary tests. He will ensure everything is good."

Kelleigh clenched her fists down by her side and gritted her teeth together. Why was Toru overruling the areas of the project she was responsible for? She had everything in place. Couriers were booked. Analysis time was scheduled in the labs.

"I need to do everything to make sure our development application is approved." Toru continues. "Without it, we're all out of a job. You understand? Yes?"

"No, I don't understand." She tugged at her shirt collar before folding her arms. "What do you mean we're out of a job?"

"Your ongoing employment is subject to the approval of the development application. If there is no approval, there's no hotel. No hotel, no job."

Kelleigh felt the color drain away from her face. She'd never considered that part of her employment agreement could ever come to fruition. She couldn't afford to be out of work; she needed the income to help pay off the debt left by Rodrigo.

Toru jutted his chin toward her. "Do I make myself clear? We have the council meeting to present our application on Wednesday week. Everything must be finalized by then. Do not waste unnecessary time on too much sampling."

Kelleigh managed to nod. Toru was her boss and she had to abide by his decisions. But if the correct sampling wasn't done, it would only create more expense down the track when construction details needed to be finalized. She couldn't work out correct foundations for all the buildings without having accurate data. What was she to do? She struggled to breathe; petrified of standing up to him, but the ability to do her job was at stake.

Why was it she could flirt and feel like she could take on the world when she was with Troy, but felt like a mouse when she was being ordered around by others? She couldn't let this happen. The consequences were too great. Her mouth ran dry as she mustered up the courage to speak. "I'm sorry, Toru, but all these samples are necessary."

Toru's nostrils flared. "We have invested a great deal of

time, effort and money into this project, we need to get this application in as soon as possible with no more delays. Do not question my authority."

Kelleigh's stomach twisted into a tight knot. Was he trying to get rid of her by making her look incompetent? Well, fuck him. That was not going to happen.

Her insides trembled and bile gurgled in her belly. Vomiting could be an option at any moment, but she held her ground. "I will question it when you don't know what you're talking about. The samples will be done as required. Nothing more. Nothing less. If you want to use Jerry, fine, but I will not cut any corners. Do I make myself clear?"

Toru's nostrils flared and his face reddened. But finally Toru nodded, very subtly, and took a step back.

"I'm glad we understand each other." Kelleigh wanted to high-five herself for finding the strength to stand up to Toru, but she was not sure she could move just yet. Everything still trembled and the knot inside her stomach hadn't gone away. She didn't trust him. Not that she trusted any man any longer, but her radar seemed to be working in overdrive when it came to Toru.

"Now we have that sorted." Toru smirked at her. *Ergh*, he was such a creep. "I need you to attend the festival dinner tomorrow night for networking purposes. We need to excite the local suppliers about the development of our new golf course and hotel. I will see you there, yes?"

What? She didn't want to go to some fancy dinner and mingle with people she didn't have anything in common with. More importantly, she didn't want to be in the same room as Toru. She searched her brain for a quick excuse. "I didn't bring anything to wear to a corporate dinner."

"Fine. Use your company credit card and go into Maitland tomorrow morning and buy yourself something. I'll authorize

$500 dollars for you to spend, is that enough?"

Five hundred dollars! The man was insane. But then she took a moment to think. She had no other plans for the weekend, and considering work offered to pay, why not take advantage of the offer. It would be a long time before she'd be able to buy anything for herself again. It had been months since she'd been out somewhere nice and had the opportunity to get dressed up nicely and go out for dinner. Pity it had to be with Toru.

"Fine. I'll go."

"I'll email you the invitation." He glanced at his watch. "I have another meeting to go to so I will see you tomorrow night at seven o'clock, yes?"

She grunted as Toru walked off down the veranda and disappeared from sight. She rolled her shoulders, glad the frosty air had now dispersed. She couldn't believe she stood up to Toru about the sampling; the glow of the small win brought a smile to her face.

She scanned over the map before her examining her sampling layout once more. Something about Toru bothered her, especially the way he acted toward Jerry. Her skin used to itch when Rodrigo told her to brush things aside, she now knew it must have been her intuition telling her he was lying and covering something up. She wasn't going to ignore the same sensation when it came to her boss. She hoped it was nothing, but couldn't let it go. At this stage it was only a hunch, but she had to follow through with the idea jumping around in her head.

Gathering up her map, she dashed off the veranda, into her Landcruiser, and headed up the hill to where her team was drilling. As she jumped out of the car, the engine on the rig roared as it resurfaced from taking another sample from the earth below. Duncan turned the motor off. Paul and Lucas detached the rod, laid out the long cylinder tube of dirt on a tray and readied to pack it into tubing for transportation.

"Wait!" Kelleigh dashed over and scanned over the sample. Looking through the layers she prayed for something to jump out at her. She hadn't paid much attention to their previous collections, but now her instinct told her otherwise. "Duncan, you got a sec?" She waved him over to the tray. "Why would Toru want us to avoid full sampling, especially where the villas and resort are to be constructed? The only thing I can think of is that there may be some form of contamination in the soil, like dangerous pesticides or something. Would there be any indication in these samples or do I have to wait for the analysis to come back?"

Duncan took off his gloves and ran his finger along the core of dirt. "Usually for chemical contamination, there's oily or black spots in the layers. Traces of pesticides aren't usually visible, they only show up in lab tests. But wait, see here. These dark patches may be something. And smell it. It doesn't quite smell earthy, does it? It's got bit of an odor."

"Right," Kelleigh said. She walked over to the truck, grabbed a new sampling rod and headed to the back of the vehicle.

"What's going on?" Duncan asked as all the men followed her. She connected the rod onto the drill and prepped the machine to dig. The rotating motor whirred loudly to life again.

"Call it women's intuition, but I don't trust Toru." She raised her voice over the noise of the engine. "For every marker, we now take two samples. One goes to Melbourne as planned, and one goes to this guy Jerry that Toru wants to use. I want to compare the results when the reports come back."

"But that's going to take us twice as long."

"Well then. We better get to it." She positioned the rod's head firmly on to the ground, slapped her hand against the button on the side of the truck and sent the drilling head into the earth below.

Chapter 17

It was nearing Friday lunchtime when Troy made his way back toward the homestead. He'd had a busy morning in the field, checking on the progress of the fruiting; this coming harvest was looking good. As he drove out of the vineyards and around the end of the wine sheds, he saw Jessica's Audi parked outside the cabins. There she stood on the porch with her eighteen-month-old baby, Liam, in her arms. Troy pulled up beside her car and jumped out to greet her. Bounding up the two steps to her side, he kissed her on her cheek. Concerned filled him as he noted her thin cheeks, the dark circles under her eyes, and her usual gorgeous tall frame looked too thin and frail.

"Hey, Jess. Good to see you as always. You okay?"

"I'm just tired. Liam still wakes up in the middle of the night and hardly sleeps through the day. All the travel we've been doing for work and organizing corporate events is exhausting. I'm looking forward to having a week off after this weekend is through."

"Sorry to say it but, yes, it looks like you need a break."

Jessica nodded as she kissed Liam on the cheek.

"May I?" Troy held out his arms to take the child.

"Sure."

Troy took the baby from Jessica and held him ever so gently, cradling him on his hip. He'd never really been around infants but took to Liam the moment he met him. Missing out on seeing his own son grow up would always remain one of the biggest regrets in his life. Holding Liam in his arms made his solar plexus ache. Liam looked so perfect as his little hands tugged at the collar of his shirt. Troy had always wanted to have kids with Nicola, but it never happened. Here was his old flame, Jessica, who had her second child at thirty-seven years of age with Nate. Maybe there was hope for him yet.

He looked down at Liam in his arm and touched the tip of his nose with a soft stroke of his fingertip. "Are you being trouble for your mummy? You wouldn't do that, would you?" he cooed at Liam.

"I've just fed him, so be careful he doesn't throw up on you."

Troy looked up when the cabin door opened and Nate appeared with a cloth.

"Hello Troy, how are you, pal? You might want this." The British hotelier offered him a cloth and placed it over his shoulder. Nate curled his arm around Jessica's waist and kissed her on the forehead; her face full of adoration as she looked up at him. Troy smiled, lost in his thoughts for a moment. Twenty years ago Jessica used to look at him like that. But a life with her was not meant to be. No second chance either; Nate had clearly won her heart. Troy held no hate, jealousy or regret toward him because the more time he spent doing business with Nate and getting to know him, the more he had to admit he was a perfect match for Jessica. Both were crazy workaholics and loved the fast-paced corporate life while he preferred to do his hard work in the outdoors and live within the serenity of the countryside.

"Thanks. I see on the Wine Festival program Jessica's reeled you in to be a keynote speaker at tomorrow night's dinner."

"Yes, she's always volunteering me to do stuff."

"While you're here I want to catch up with you. Our new semillons are ready and I want to discuss the possibility of expanding our supply into your hotels. Our wine continues to do very well in your restaurant in Sydney."

"Sure," Nate agreed. "My food and beverage manager is coming up for the day tomorrow. If your wine is as good as you say it is we may consider putting more through our Asian and European hotels. I know it's a busy weekend for you; when's the best time to catch up?"

For Gumtrees to expand their supply into Nate's hotel chain internationally was the opportunity Troy was looking for. More sales, more revenue and more recognition. The additional income would benefit their new projects starting after harvest. Troy's schedule was busy during the festival tomorrow, but Sunday was clear. "How about first thing on Sunday morning? Nine o'clock in the restaurant?"

"Sounds grand." Nate replied in his strong British accent. "We've got to head back to Sydney early in the afternoon, so that would suit me well."

Troy grinned, unable to hide his enthusiasm.

For no apparent reason, Liam burst out crying. Troy lay Liam over his shoulder and patted his back. He tried rocking, rubbing, whispering and everything he could think of to settle him down, but his sobs were getting worse.

Feeling helpless, he glanced over at Jessica for help. Her shoulders slumped and her face was drawn with exhaustion. "Why don't you go and have a rest," he said to her, "I'll take him for a walk over to see the horses."

"I'm fine. I don't need a rest. Here, let me take him." Jessica held out her hands to take the baby but Liam reached out for Nate.

Nate took Liam in his arms. "Jess, why don't you go for a walk with Troy and catch up. You said you wanted to stretch your legs after the long drive. I'll take Liam inside and see if I can get him down for a sleep."

As Liam curled in to Nate's chest he immediately started to settle. It reaffirmed to Troy he was definitely not father material. Nate took the cloth from Troy's shoulder, but not quickly enough. With one almighty belch that most men would be proud off, Liam threw up all over Nate's shoulder. Troy couldn't help but laugh.

"Bollocks!" Nate cursed. "Why do you always do that on me?" Liam's face beamed with the widest of grins. "Let's go and get cleaned up." Nate didn't look impressed as he turned on his heels and headed inside the cabin.

"Well Jess, would you mind if I joined you for a walk or would you prefer to go by yourself and enjoy the peace and quiet?"

"I'd love you to join me. It's been too long since we've caught up face to face. Let's go."

With no further prompts required, Troy offered out his arm. She curled hers around his as he led her down the steps toward the front vineyard.

Within a matter of fifty yards, the tension in Jessica's arms faded away and the stress disappeared from her face. She only glanced over her shoulder once to make sure Nate didn't need her help.

"I've loved hearing from you about all the big things happening at Gumtrees." Jessica started. "More weddings. New business. It all sounds so exciting. What else has been going on that I don't know about? It's still hard to believe you're now a joint owner of my Gumtrees!"

He chuckled. *Her Gumtrees!* Her R&R getaway from Sydney had played its part in reuniting them. When he told her about buying into Gumtrees, she had taken a while to get used to the news. This place was very dear to her. She'd long considered it her home away from home. It took him a long time to convince her he felt the same: this was his home and where he belonged.

"All our expansion plans are finalized. Conner has done some amazing designs for the new function room and accommodation cabins and we've sourced a local builder. It will be sad to see the old barn and yards go, but it's time to spruce the place up. I've also planned to put another few acres under vine next year. We've a busy year ahead."

Jessica's face distorted and displayed a broad array of emotions. Happy. Sad. Excited. Confused. He didn't know what to make of it. "I can't believe you had a hidden businessman inside you all along."

"Ha! No," Troy shook his head. "Nick is the businessman, Maria orders us around and I'm the worker."

"Well, whatever you three are doing it seems to be working."

"I know this place means a lot to you, Jess. And it means everything to me. It led me to finding Conner and has finally given me purpose again." He cleared his throat. "By the way, have you talked to Conner lately?"

"Yeah, why? What's up? He should be here soon."

"About his work situation? I offered him the opportunity to come and work here. I know you offered him a job as well, but I wanted to put another option on the table for him to consider. Coming into harvest it's really busy around here and the option to stay on is there if he wants."

Jessica's hand shot up to cover her mouth and her eyes swelled with tears. It took her a moment before she could speak. "No, he didn't tell me. But that's wonderful news. I'll support him in whatever he decides to do. I just wish he'd hurry up and do something with his life. Thank you. Thank you so much."

The air was knocked out of his lungs when Jessica flung her

arms around his chest and hugged him tightly. He hesitated, then wrapped his arms around her. He rested his chin on her shoulder as they embraced.

"What's that smell?" Jessica inhaled deeply near his neck.

He withdrew back from her embrace. "What smell?"

"That? On your collar." She pointed at his neck. "It smells like perfume."

Troy flushed and rubbed the side of his neck with the palm of his hand, like trying to rub off a pen mark accidently drawn on your skin. "Nothing."

Jessica's eyes narrowed. Only she could glare like that and make his insides flip with guilt.

"I know the smell of your cologne and it doesn't smell anything like that. Is there something else you want to tell me?" A smile twitched at the corner of her mouth.

He looked around everywhere, trying to avoid her stare. But there would be no point in denying it; she could read him like an open book. "With all the rain yesterday, I didn't get any work done outside, so I just wore the same shirt today. Sorry, does it smell bad?"

"No, no, no. It's not sweat. It smells of ladies' perfume. Is your feminine side coming out?"

He fidgeted with his collar. "That's definitely not the case."

She playfully slapped him on the arm. "Tell me everything. Who is she? Someone I know from around here?"

He shoved his hands into the back pockets of his jeans. "There's not much to tell. She's someone here on a short-term project. One thing led to another. Well, actually it's been twice now. But that's it."

He'd been trying not to think of Kelleigh. Yesterday had turned out to be one afternoon in the cellar he'd never forget. However, having to explain to Nick why thirty minutes of security footage was deleted from their logs was nothing short of embarrassing. Nick had tears running down his face from laughing so much. Luckily Kelleigh had not been there at the time.

"Good for you." She said as they continued to head down through the trellises where the vines were weighed down with heavy bunches of grapes near ready for picking. "I told you you'd meet someone new. I was thinking someone a little more long-term. But hey, gotta start somewhere, right?"

"She's nice. But temporary."

"Now that sounds familiar. That's what Nate was supposed to be as well. Look what happened to us. Married. A baby. International jet-setting lifestyle firmly established. So don't go writing off the possibility with someone if you like her."

He was trying not to like her. Trying to ignore the way he felt when she was in the room. Trying to get her out of his mind.

Troy shook his head. "It's nothing serious. She's from Melbourne anyway. Besides, I'm not looking for a relationship."

"Why not? You're a great catch." She looked at him with concern.

He hesitated as he looked out over the horizon. It didn't matter that he liked Kelleigh, he couldn't open his heart up to the prospect of love. "You of all people know what I've been through. Unlucky in love, that's me. Now Gumtrees and Conner fill my purpose in life."

"Ha ... that's what I thought after I divorced Graeme. Drowned myself in work to numb the pain. Figured my chances of finding love again were slim to none, but the universe can conspire in mysterious ways. After what I've been through, I wouldn't rule out anything. You're a handsome man, Troy Smith. Don't lock yourself away from the prospect of finding someone to make you happy."

"Words from the wise, hey?" He'd like to have Jessica's optimism, but he was too much of a realist.

"How's Larry?" She looked out across the foothills toward his property.

"Not too good. He hasn't been well since winter. Would you believe his place is up for a conditional sale to a company that wants to turn it into a golf course and resort hotel? I'm not sure if Maxine has told you, but I've been talking to her about trying to find a legal way to stop it from going ahead. She hasn't been able to come up with anything for me yet."

"Yeah, she mentioned it. Max is ruthless; she'll find something."

Troy was hopeful but his chances were getting slimmer by the day. He had ten days before the rezoning meeting and had nothing that would put a halt on the project.

"It's getting late, I'd better head back." Jessica said as they reached the end of one of the vineyard rows. Turning around, they meandered back up the slope toward the cabins. "Conner's staying with you, right?" Jessica enquired. "I'll come and see him later on at your cottage if that's all right? He's supposed to be helping me out tomorrow and I need to run through his tasks. Your presentation is at one o'clock in the afternoon, straight after lunch. Then are you still able to come to the dinner?"

Jessica was like a well-oiled machine, she never stopped. Her attention to detail and meticulous planning in running corporate events had led her to be very successful.

"Of course, I'll be there. Even going to wear a suit for you."

Chapter 18

Kelleigh walked into the crowded function room on Saturday night at the Hunter Valley Crowne Plaza Hotel; the sea of unfamiliar faces bewildered her. The golden carpet stretched out before her. Black-covered chairs with golden sashes and tables dressed with elaborate centerpiece decorations awaited all the dinner guests in the vast ballroom. In the pre-function area hundreds of people mingled around bar tables, while wait staff navigated successfully through the sea of bodies with trays full of beverages. Among all this glitz and glamor, Kelleigh didn't recognize anyone. Her boss was supposed to be here but was nowhere to be found.

She smoothed her hands down over the black lace of her new cocktail dress and then brushed her hands through her new short shoulder-length haircut. She was still not used to the light feel of it after having her long black hair cut off and dyed blonde at the hairdressers in Maitland today. Such a bold change, but one that she needed. The new her was slowly coming to life.

Straightening her stance, she made her way over to a vacant

bar table and grabbed a glass of champagne from one of the waiters as she walked passed. Taking a seat, she took a sip of her bubbles and surveyed the room, wondering why the hell she was here.

In all her rushing around today, Kelleigh forgot to call her sister. She grabbed her phone from her new clutch to send a quick message. As she started to type, she caught sight of Toru talking to Jerry in the shadows off to the side of the room. The hairs on the back of her neck stood up, prickling her skin when she saw Toru reach into his suit jacket pocket and hand Jerry a thick, yellow envelope.

Kelleigh's brain clicked into action. She swiped her phone over to the camera app and took a picture of the two men, just as Jerry accepted the envelope. What the hell was going on? Was this what Toru meant when he said he would do anything to ensure that the development was approved? Kelleigh sat dumbfounded, wondering if her suspicions were correct. Was there something of concern on Larry's place? Her heart raced and her hands trembled as she quickly put her phone away when Toru started to approach her.

"Was that Jerry? What were you two talking about?" She tried to sound aloof, while her palms sweated profusely against the satin fabric of her clutch.

"I wanted to ensure our reports will be ready on time for our meeting with council."

"What did you hand him?" she asked, before taking a quick sip on her champagne.

Toru drew out his handkerchief and wiped his brow. "I don't know what you're talking about."

Kelleigh glared at him; frustration formed a knot between her shoulder blades. She wasn't able to ignore her suspicions. "I saw you hand him an envelope. What was in it? Was it money?"

"That's none of your concern. I'm doing what is necessary

to ensure our reports are good." He stuffed his hanky back in his pocket and did up his jacket button. "You are concocting things out of nothing. Maybe too much champagne, yes?"

Kelleigh shook her head. "I've had one sip. I know what I saw."

"You saw nothing, Miss Johnstone. Now, please excuse me, I have other guests to meet. See you at dinner. Yes?"

Toru turned on his heels and disappeared into the crowd. Kelleigh waited until he was out of view before she reached into her clutch and turned off the voice record button on her cell phone. Staring at the screen, she couldn't believe she held damning evidence that Toru was corrupt. But what should she do with it?

After grabbing another glass of champagne, she slid off her chair and made her way outside for some fresh air on the terrace. She needed to think straight and decide what to do about Toru. She wondered if head office in Japan was behind these actions. Was Toru just doing his job? Was it money in the envelope or something else? Maybe it really was nothing and she should let it slide. She placed her hand on her tummy and rubbed it. No, there was an unsettled feeling in the pit of her stomach that meant something was wrong. She'd have to wait until the reports came back to see if her instinct was right.

Heading back inside, she stopped in the doorway; her attention was drawn to the main doorway. Her breath hitched when she saw Troy walk in to the room. He was with other people, but she didn't care about them. He looked up and caught her gaze. Those sapphire eyes made her forget there was a world existing around her. A smile tugged at the corner of his lips before he excused himself and approached her. Her knees weakened as she glanced over his suited attire. Broad shoulders and toned arms filled out the black outfit in all the right places. She couldn't decide which outfit made him look more handsome; this one, or his worn-out Akubra hat and faded blue jeans. She'd settle for either, but the latter was more suited to him. She raised her eyebrow when he stopped in front of her; impressed at how fine he scrubbed up for the occasion. Damn her stupid heart as it thudded in her chest.

"You look amazing," he swooned, leaning in to kiss her on the cheek. "Yet again, our paths have crossed." His eyed drifted over her, shimmering with desire. "Did you think by changing your hairstyle I wouldn't recognize you? I don't think there's anything you could do that wouldn't capture my attention." The deep tone of his voice rippled through her body, seeping through her veins like a cup of hot, delicious cocoa. "You were beautiful before, now I think I'm going to have to put you in the class of breathtaking."

She blushed at his appraisal. "The country air must be getting to me. It's making me go all natural, even back to my original hair color." She smiled sheepishly as she ruffled her hand through her hairdo.

"It suits you. Makes you look even sexier."

Mm, so did he. All cleanly shaven. Smelling of a spicy cologne. Handsome as hell in a dinner suit.

"Thank you." She glanced down to the floor, embarrassed by his compliment and consciously trying not to ogle at him for too long.

"I wasn't expecting to see you here this evening." From the grin on his face he didn't looked disappointed.

"I wasn't expecting you either; you said you were only doing a talk today." He shook his head, unable to hide his smile, making butterflies flutter in her tummy. "My boss is here and insisted I come and network. But these people are all suppliers, wholesalers and restaurant and hotel chains, I have nothing in common with them."

"You're here with your boss?" He balked, stiffening his

stance.

She choked on a mouthful of her drink. "Yes, but not as his partner, if that's what you're implying. Strictly business. The more I can avoid him the better. He's far from my favorite person at the moment."

His shoulders relaxed, a glint of charm returned to his eyes as he straightened his tie. "Uh-ha, I think you're just looking for more excuses to see me. But if you really don't want to be with your boss, would you like to join me at our table for dinner? We have a spare seat because my son has decided to go off drinking with friends at Harrigan's rather than stay here."

She blinked. "What did you say? I didn't know you have a son. How old is he if he's out drinking?" Troy didn't look old enough to have a grown son.

"Conner. He's twenty-two."

"Wow," she gasped. She should've expected him to have kids at his age. He'd been married after all. "It must've been hard for you raising him after losing your wife." She couldn't think of anything worse. In spite of their differences, she was really close to her family. Then she thought of Rodrigo. Thank God she never had kids with him. What a horrendous father figure he would've been. He had no morals. No values. No respect.

"I didn't." Troy's voice lowered. "His mother, Jessica raised him. Unfortunately he grew up without me. I only found out about him when I came back from the States a few years ago."

She closed her eyes for a second to stop her mind from boggling. "I thought you said Nicola was your wife. So who, where and how does Jessica fit in to the picture?"

Troy held up his finger to attract the attention of a waiter walking past with a tray of drinks and grabbed a beer. Taking a sip, he licked his lips before he spoke.

"I think I mentioned to you that Jessica's the event manager behind tonight. She was my girlfriend back in high school. I didn't know she was pregnant with Conner when I left to live overseas." Regret flashed in his eyes, it was obviously a hard topic for him to talk about. "You will meet her if you join me at our table. Her husband Nate Somers is here as well."

"Nate Somers. Really?" She rolled the stem of her glass between her fingertips as she contemplated his offer. "Are you sure? Who else is with you?"

If yet again some force beyond her control had led her to see Troy again, why try and fight it. More importantly, she didn't want to. Not tonight. Maybe the champagne was starting to take effect, but she'd sooner spend time with him, Nick and Maria who hated JLR, and others she'd never met than be near her boss.

"A few of the staff from Gumtrees. This is a big night for us. We're up for two awards."

"I don't want to intrude on your group."

"You won't be. Please join me."

Her boss insisted she network, so surely this would fall into that category. Seeing Troy again, all dressed up in a dinner suit, looking at her with such intensity, was causing her body temperature to rise and had her doubting her self-control. Would she be able to keep her hands to herself?

Oh, what the hell. "I'd love to."

Resting his hand against the small of her back, Troy guided her over to his table. With every step she took, she was drawn closer and closer into his side. Close enough to slip her hand around his waist, but he took hold of it instead. Clearing his throat, he stumbled over his words when he introduced her to everyone at the table. Nate and Jessica beamed with charisma, while Nick, Maria and the Gumtrees staff eyed her suspiciously as Troy helped her to take the seat next to him.

"Is it hot in here, or is it me in this damn jacket?" Troy flapped the side of his lapels to cool off.

As dinner commenced, everyone made her feel welcome; falling into conversation and laughing about work, travel, the pending harvest and upcoming events. This group of strangers felt more like friends to her than anyone she'd known for years back in Melbourne.

Every now and then, in her peripheral vision, she caught sight of Troy gazing at her when she spoke. It was hard to resist the temptation to slip her hand underneath the table and place it on his leg. She wanted to touch him. Every time she thought about it, she saw a cheeky look in his eye, or that smile that touched the corner of his lips. She wondered if he was thinking the exact same thing.

Alternate meals were served to the table with prompt efficiency and Kelleigh giggled as she watched Troy enjoy the fusion of flavors as he ate his meal. The little noises and groans he made with every mouthful made it look like the most amazing dish ever. She longed to kiss his lips, taste his mouth and share in the indulgence.

If only.

"Mmm ... you have to taste this." Troy cut a bite-sized piece from his portion of beef and held it toward her. She was caught off guard by the offer but wasn't about to refuse. She leaned toward him, opened her mouth and let him slide the fork into her mouth.

The food was delicious.

"Was that your way of getting me to offer you some of mine?" She pointed to the quail dish in front of her.

"Absolutely. Fair's fair." He edged closer to her. How could she refuse?

She speared a piece on to her fork, smothered it in the jus and offered it to his eagerly awaiting mouth.

"That's pretty good," he said as he licked his lips, but then leaned over and whispered in her ear. "Not as good as having you in the wine cellar."

Kelleigh dropped her knife and it clattered loudly on her plate. Her eyes darted up to find Jessica and Nate, Nick and Maria staring at her and Troy. Surely they hadn't heard his comment. No, it had to be about the food. Was that a sparkle in Jessica's eye as she smiled in Troy's direction? Nate looked mortified by their bad table manners. What was she thinking of sharing her food like that with Troy? It was rude at such an event, but hey, he'd started it. Oh, she wanted to crawl under the table and hide in shame.

The emcee drew their attention, bringing some relief to Kelleigh, and commenced the announcement of the awards. Champagne bottles popped loudly when Gumtrees walked away with Semillon Wine of the Year for the second year running, and celebrations continued into the night.

Placing her hand on her hot cheek, Kelleigh felt flushed from too much champagne.

"Shall we dance?" Troy offered out his hand.

"I'm not much of a dancer, I have two left feet," Kelleigh hated to admit she was unable to keep time to a beat.

"Well, I have two right feet, so maybe together we'll make a perfect match."

Not taking no for an answer, he stood up and led her on to the dance floor. Jostling in among the crowd, he weaved one hand around her waist while the other took hers and held it against his chest. Music streamed around them, making her heart thud in time with the rock beat. Twirling around together, Troy's eyes stayed locked on to hers, undeterred by the shuffling crowd surrounding them.

"Congratulations once again on your win." Kelleigh swayed side to side from the buzz of the champagne and concentrated on balancing on her high heels. "What does it do for your business?"

"We get a special gold sticker to put on our wine bottles." He chuckled. "But on a serious note, it does wonders in publicity. We'll get some great write-ups and hopefully pick up a few new supply contracts with more restaurants and wholesalers."

"More grand plans." she said, unable to hide the sharp tone in her voice and accidently stepped on his right toe. "I'm sorry. I didn't mean to be rude. It's just that my ex was always in to some scheme."

Unaffected by her misstep, he held her tight to ensure she maintained her balance. "Don't be silly. You're fine. This is everyday business for us. To have a market demanding our wines is good. It benefits all areas of our operation. Accommodation occupancy rates go up, the restaurant becomes more popular, and more suppliers take on our wine. Nick and I have been in the wine industry for a long time and we like to think we know what we're doing. We don't have any grand plans to take on the world. We want to stay small and boutique. We're sensible about what we do ... most of the time anyway."

She rested her chin on Troy's shoulder; the cotton of his shirt brushing softly against her skin. Sensible was not how her heart was reacting or why her body was aching for more of his touch.

She turned and looked into his sapphire eyes. "I wish you every success with Gumtrees. You have a great bunch of people to work with."

"It's a lot of hard work and these people are my family; I'd do anything for them."

He rubbed his hand up and down her back, molding his body next to hers as they continued around the dance floor. She closed her eyes, savoring every moment. He felt so strong. So safe. So heavenly.

"You have so much to look forward to, I think I am envious. All I have is my sister's baby due soon and my job." Providing the development for the resort was approved and she remained employed.

"Sounds like you have a lot going for you, if you ask me."

Life could be worse. Not much worse, but worse. She couldn't stay living in this bubble out in the Hunter Valley forever, but going home scared her. Having to face her reality again and the thought of never experiencing these feelings or seeing Troy again was not something she looked forward to.

The soft brush of his fingertips against her cheek caused her to glance up.

"Hey, what's wrong?" Captivated by his enchanting blue eyes, she fell further under his hypnotic spell.

"It's getting late. I'm tired and my feet are killing me in these shoes. I'm struggling to find the strength to say goodbye to you yet again."

"Then don't."

"What did you say?" she whispered.

"My tie is strangling me. I have a blister on my heel from wearing these dress shoes but I don't want to stop dancing with you because I don't want to let you go. Let me take you home. Let me make love to you. Let me share your bed again before we have to part ways."

Her heart lurched, knowing her feelings for him were forging deeper and deeper into her heart.

She closed her eyes. She'd be foolish not to walk away and leave now; even more foolish to say yes.

Then she opened her eyes and saw the look. The one she'd longed for. The one of such intensity it reached deep inside her and touched her very soul. How was her heart ever going to survive this?

He nuzzled into her neck, breathed in her perfume, kissed her beneath her lobe. "One more night. Say you want me to stay with you."

Her lips parted, goose bumps shot down her arm. She couldn't think straight and, more importantly, she didn't want to.

Kelleigh entwined her fingers with his and nodded. Following her temptation out through the crowd, they gathered their belongings from the table and headed out the door.

Chapter 19

The days disappeared too quickly. Kelleigh worked long hours with her team in the scorching summer sun. A long cool shower at the end of each day to rid herself of all the sweat and dirt was her form of heaven.

She had to keep herself busy to keep her mind occupied. Otherwise all she did was think about Troy. She hadn't seen him since he left her room on Sunday morning. Four days had passed with only a few little text messages and the odd wave from him as she drove down to Larry's and he happened to be working in the section of the vineyard near the road. Considering she was leaving in a week's time, keeping contact to a minimum probably was for the best.

Her team had kept with her grueling schedule and taken all the extra samples as requested. And as the rain set in again on Thursday afternoon, the last batch of extractions was sent off for testing. One lot to Jerry, the other to Melbourne.

All she had left to do was to finalize the surveying, attend the council rezoning meeting on Wednesday and then she would be able to head home at the end of next week.

Standing in the middle of the paddock with her crew, the rain's intensity grew, hindering their visibility and making it impossible to work on the surveying. Looking up at the darkened sky, it didn't look like it was going to clear any time soon. With everyone soaked through, she called it a day and sent her team home early. All she wanted was a bit of sunshine so she could finish this job and head home. She missed Franny and looked forward to catching up with her.

But Mother Nature had her own ideas. More and more rain fell on Friday and across the entire weekend. Inches of rain drenched the earth. The creeks were swollen and the paddocks a muddy bog when Kelleigh managed to get back out to Larry's on Monday morning. Traipsing through waist-high green grass and two inches of mud in the sticky humidity was hot and uncomfortable work. The tripods kept sinking or moving in the mud, making it difficult to gather accurate survey readings. But she and her team persevered and made slow but steady progress. The hard work kept her from thinking about Friday. Four days until she'd be heading home and no chance of ever seeing Troy again.

***

Kelleigh's eyes shot open the next morning. Crap, it was nearly eight o'clock. Somehow the alarm clock had failed to go off and she'd slept in.

Pulling on her hi-vis gear and doing up her steel-caps in record time, she quickly sat down in front of her laptop to check her email before heading out for the day.

She skimmed through all of her messages until she found one she'd been waiting for. It was the environmental audit, soil and water results. But this one was Jerry's, not the one from Melbourne. *Bugger!* She opened the attached Excel spreadsheet and scanned through the data.

Her brow furrowed as she read the mineral analysis in the report. Damn it. There was nothing irregular in the document. And that concerned her. There were no traces of anything, which was highly unusual for agricultural farmland used for growing produce. Larry's place was full of rich, beautiful soil, but this report indicated that it was of poor quality and useless for growing anything. How could that be?

This report swayed the development application in JLR's favor. That was a good thing, right? It meant she'd keep her job and so did her team. The golf course and hotel would go ahead as planned.

But the niggling sensation returned to her belly and grew stronger and stronger. Tapping her fingers on the desk, she prayed the report from Melbourne would come through to her before the council meeting tomorrow. She needed to compare the two. If the reports were the same, she could stop with all this worry and suspicion. If the Melbourne analysis didn't come through in time, there'd be nothing she could do to prove that Toru was up to no good.

With all the feasibility studies completed, the JLR development application was ready for submission. Troy and the surrounding farmers would be devastated to know it looked like the project would proceed. She was glad she wouldn't be around to see the disappointment on his face.

While on one hand she didn't want to lose her job, on the other hand, if this report from Jerry was concocted, she wanted to take Toru down. The legal ramifications for JLR in the future could be astronomical.

Worried about time, her job and her team, her intuition was playing havoc with her mind. She wiggled her fingers above the keyboard, wondering what to do.

Troy needed to see this report. Maybe there was something

in it she was missing. She hoped not. She clicked on the forward button and typed in Troy's email address from the business card she'd received at her first meeting at Gumtrees. With a quick message she indicated the results were all clear and the project was viable before she hit the send button.

Grabbing her keys, she set off to Larry's for another day of work. Surveying of the land was the only remaining task to be completed for the future construction.

***

Troy sat in his office checking his email messages before he had to start scheduling the labor hire for the up and coming harvest. Employing workers to handpick some of the older vines was not his favorite task. It was time consuming and would keep his mind from thinking about Kelleigh working over in Larry's fields.

Spending the festival dinner with her had made it one of the most memorable evenings he'd had in a long time. Staying the night with her a wonderful unexpected turn of events. Keeping his distance from her was hard, knowing she was still here. He was trying to be sensible knowing she was leaving.

As he read through his inbox, his eyes widened when he saw a message from Kelleigh. He opened it and leaned in for a closer look. She'd sent him a copy of the environmental audit and sampling report. Why? Clicking on the attachment, he opened the document and skimmed through the executive summary. Every word he read felt like another weight was placed on his shoulder. *Damn it!* It looked like there was nothing in the report that would halt the development. Clicking through the pages, all the words started to blend together and the technical jargon made his head hurt. Then he reached the section consisting of the soil sampling result and perused over the list of mineral levels and trace elements. Nothing unusual. *Bugger.* He stopped scrolling and was about to close the document down when it struck him that something wasn't right.

His eyes rescanned down the columns of figures on the screen. There it was. In plain black and white. Actually, it wasn't there at all. To double-check, he stood up, took two long strides over to his filing cabinet, yanked it open and withdrew the folder of the water and soil tests performed on Gumtrees over the past several years. He found the results for the area closest to Larry's farm. He skimmed over the figures in his data and compared them to the figures in Kelleigh's report. Back and forth he went. The two documents were miles apart. How could Larry's farm be so vastly different from Gumtrees? He knew the data would be slightly different due to different farming practices, but such extremities were not possible.

Falling back into his chair, he coursed his fingers through his hair. Wasn't Kelleigh the one responsible for supervising the environmental audit? How had the consultant's analysis come up with these results? She wouldn't have sent him a copy of this report if she didn't approve it, would she? A lump formed in his throat and he swallowed hard as a bitter taste rose in his mouth. Had ... had she doctored the figures? The very notion made his fists clench and jaw strain as he stared at his screen. Hurt, disappointment and anger burned inside his chest. Was this what she was really like? She'd lied to him from the start, not telling him why she'd come to town, not giving him any indication of who she was or who she worked for. Now this. Did she lie about everything?

He slammed his fist down on the desk, making every pen, pencil and notepad jump. He'd actually liked her and thought she was a decent human being, but no, she was ruthless. Just like Jessica who would do anything for her business. Just like Nicola with all the lies and manipulation.

He thought he'd seen the real Kelleigh and understood her. How wrong had he been? How foolish was he for falling back into her bed? He wasn't usually one to get worked up about anything, but this report infuriated him.

He had to find out the truth. He grabbed his phone off the desk and called Kelleigh's number. Had he been right all along and should have stayed away from her? His time with her was going to be tarnished once again. Listening to the dial tone, he swore when it went straight to message bank.

Kelleigh was not going to get away with this.

Flicking through his contacts, he dialed Maxine.

"Hey Max, I may have found something for you and Ray to look at regarding this whole debacle at Larry's. The project leader, Kelleigh, sent me their environmental audit results and they are vastly different to our tests conducted here at Gumtrees. Something doesn't add up."

"Send it through. We don't have much time before the meeting tomorrow. I'll jump on it straightaway. I was about to meet with Ray to finalize everything before we come up tomorrow. We're confident we're going to win. Without the acquisition of the surrounding neighbor's properties, there's no viable economic and social benefit to the community. We're also strongly opposing the rezoning due to the agricultural use of the land. Don't stress. A report that doesn't match up just means the council may rule for a third party to do another assessment—it's not a strong enough case by itself, but every bit helps.

Troy wished he had Maxine's confidence. He wouldn't rest until JLR and Kelleigh were gone from the Hunter Valley for good.

"I'll email it to you straight away. Looking forward to seeing you at the meeting tomorrow."

Chapter 20

Rain fell in heavy curtains across the Valley on Wednesday morning as Troy rushed into the council's office. Maxine, with her hair pulled back in a tight bun, designer suit and lethal-looking high heels, stood next to Ray, who donned a conservative black suit. Both looked like stereotypical intimidating lawyers as they waited for him in the foyer.

"Good to see you, Max, it's been a while." Troy said over a handshake. "Ray, nice to meet you."

"You ready to stop a golf course?" Maxine asked with a sparkle in her eye. "I fucking love this shit. You good to go?"

Troy and Ray nodded as Maxine led them into the meeting room. Troy's nerves edged up a notch when he saw Toru and another man in a stiff-looking suit he assumed to be with JLR. A couple of men from the council sat at the head of the table, flicking through documents and papers that lay before them.

"Hey Troy, glad you made it on time." Matthew, one of the council members greeted him with a firm handshake. Hopefully being on friendly terms with one of the men on the review panel worked in his favor.

"Hey Matt. This is Maxine Gordon and Ray Whistler, my lawyers from Sydney."

The team for JLR reluctantly shook hands and introduced themselves before taking seats again.

"I was not made aware of others being involved in this meeting," Toru interjected.

Matt waved his pen. "Yes you were. I've emailed numerous communications stating this is an open meeting regarding your application to rezone an area of the Valley. As a neutral body we have to review both sides of the equation and do our own investigations before we make our decision."

Troy concealed a snigger as Toru wiped his brow with his handkerchief. He wanted the man to sweat and squirm.

The door burst open and Kelleigh entered with a rush, carrying an armful of documents. "Sorry I'm late, I was waiting for some files to print."

Every muscle in Troy's body went rigid as he watched her take her seat. Firstly, she wasn't supposed—she clearly stated from the beginning she wouldn't be involved in any of the legalities regarding this case. Secondly, since receiving the email from her yesterday, he'd been unable to talk to her. She didn't return his phone calls, didn't message him or come and see him after work, which seemed to confirm his suspicions. Her eyes darted around the room and she fidgeted with everything in sight as she settled at the table. He glared at her. He'd been foolish to think for a moment that there had been a spark between them. Foolish to believe Jessica when she said that there was hope for everyone to fall in love again. No, that moment of weakness for Kelleigh had gone and now it was down to business.

The meeting proceeded as Toru started to present the results of their initial studies. Aboriginal Archaeology assessment all cleared, Bushfire Threat cleared. Social and economic development would boost tourism in the area. The list went on and on and Troy's heart sank, sure that his efforts to stop the development would be futile.

Then it was Maxine and Ray's turn to deliver their findings. Traffic and Infrastructure costs would be exorbitant. Without the neighboring properties agreeing to sell, JLR would not have enough land for a fully integrated tourist project; therefore, as a standalone golf course and hotel, it wouldn't provide enough financial benefit to the community. The current zoning is and should remain agricultural as the property was surrounded by prime viticulture land.

"And for your information, we have provided a summary of recent water and soil tests done on Gumtrees and have concerns about the accuracy and detail of the trace elements detailed in their submitted report." Maxine handed the documentation to Matthew.

Maxine might exude confidence but Troy knew their chances of success were slim. As Matthew flicked through the summaries of the reports in front of him, all hope seemed lost. Then Kelleigh interrupted the proceedings. Her hands trembled as she handed everyone a new printout and her voice faltered as she spoke.

"While we are on this subject, yes, the report provided by Toru is incorrect. I have a new one here to present."

Troy gave her an evil stare. What now? Was this more damning evidence to ensure the project was approved? Reluctantly, he picked up the document.

"Kelleigh," Toru jumped in and waved his hands around. "I'm sure Jerry provided an accurate report; there is no error."

Kelleigh took a deep breath. She looked like she was about to vomit. "No Toru. I have worked in engineering and site analysis for years and know what I am talking about. The geo-tech report of Jerry's is missing vital information. I had samples sent to another lab for testing to compare the results. The report from our consultants in Melbourne came through this morning and it clearly indicates there are high traces of pesticides in the soil."

Troy shook his head. He couldn't believe what he was hearing. Was she jeopardizing her own project? Why?

"No, you are wrong, Miss Johnstone." Toru's face was turning red as he tugged on his tie. "Their report must be wrong, not Jerry's."

"I'm positive it's not. And I'm sure that document from Gumtrees will support these finds. In many of the samples we took on the foothills we found dark patches of concern in the rods. It wasn't until the results came back my suspicions were confirmed. There are traces of DDT—dichlorodiphenyltrichloroethane, Aldrin and Dieldrin. These pesticides are all now banned, but because the chemicals don't break down they are still evident in the soil. While they have minimal impact to farming, human exposure can lead to serious illness," she addressed all of her findings to the attendees.

"You don't know what you are talking about," Toru let out a strained laugh.

Troy wanted to kick himself under the table. He should have thought of this. Of course, before the ban in the late 80s these pesticides were used everywhere in the Valley.

But did Kelleigh know what she was doing? She was putting her project at risk. This moved the scales for halting the development in his direction. He didn't know whether he wanted to kiss her or shake some sense into her. Was this courage or downright stupidity on her part? She had some guts whatever the case, and that was something to admire.

"I do know, Toru. This audit suggests that the site is too high-risk to build on. Land sculpting and the construction of the hotel and villas will result in too much exposure and risk to humans."

"Miss Johnstone, that's enough." Toru's eyes looked like they were going to pop out of his head.

Kelleigh ignored him and turned to the councilmen. "Matthew, you can order another audit if you wish, but I am sure those reports from Gumtrees that Troy's lawyers provided will support these findings."

Troy sat stunned in his seat. Kelleigh had just provided the most crucial piece of evidence to prevent the development. This was incredible. He knew those reports she sent were suspect. He collapsed back in his chair while Toru and their lawyer could provide no justifiable explanation.

What a turn of events.

"Is that everything then?" Matthew asked as he gathered all the documentation from everyone. "We'll review all this information along with the application and call you if we have any enquiries. We should be able to make a decision by tomorrow morning."

Everyone said their goodbyes and headed outside into the foyer.

As Troy walked out behind Max and Ray, he saw Toru having words with Kelleigh just outside the door. Toru's face was flaming red and Kelleigh looked undoubtedly upset by whatever he was saying. Before he could react, she dashed into the rain across the car park. The urge to run after her made him ache all over, but he had to stay and thank his lawyers.

"That went well. I think we kicked their fucking asses," Maxine grinned, looking very pleased with herself. "Kelleigh just handed the ruling to us on a silver plate. The council would be crazy to approve this application. Trust me; they won't want to risk future law suits."

"There's no way this will be approved," Ray said. "If it is, we'll take it to the next level. It's a guaranteed win. I bet my life on it."

Troy smiled, absorbing their positive vibe. But his mind was elsewhere as they exited the building. He saw Kelleigh sitting in her Landcruiser, head down on the steering wheel. When she sat upright, she wiped her cheeks with her fingertips. Damn it, she was crying. He needed to get to her. Find out what was wrong. Thank her for all she had done. He excused himself from Max and Ray and stepped out into the rain to cross the car park to her. But it was too late. She took off before he could reach her. He was left standing, rain drenching him through to his skin, unable to do anything other than watch her go.

"Looks like she can't get out of town fast enough." Ray laughed as Troy returned to stand under the awning of the building.

Troy tried to join in Ray's joke, but he was worried about Kelleigh. He had questions, wanted answers, and wanted to thank her. Basically, he was looking for any excuse to see her again before she left.

"I think this calls for lunch." said Maxine, "Somewhere with lots of fine wine. Where to, Troy?"

Bugger. He couldn't fob them off, not after all the hard work they'd done for him in such a short period of time. Lunch it was, then he'd go in search of Kelleigh.

***

"Good news." Maxine said to Troy and Nick on speakerphone the following morning. "JLR's request for development has been denied. We've just received notice from Matthew. The council wouldn't approve the application for rezoning because the land must remain an agricultural property and those trace elements have them running scared. They'll do anything to avoid being sued. I think another major factor is that without acquiring the neighboring acres, the golf course wouldn't generate enough jobs, tourism and income for the community. It's a huge win for us."

Troy and Nick slapped each other a high-five and sighed in relief.

"Max, you're the best. I owe you one." Troy said with true sincerity.

"Too fucking right. I'll hold you to that. But Ray did most of the work. This was his area of expertise."

"Thanks, Ray." You couldn't wipe the smile off Nick's face if you tried. Troy felt his was just as broad.

"You're welcome." Ray's voice boomed down the phone line.

After jokes about bills and legal fees to pay, Troy hung up and punched the air, celebrating their triumph. No golf course. No hotel. No villas. Life couldn't get much better with such a win.

But what about Kelleigh? He'd been unable to find her yesterday afternoon. She wasn't at Harrigan's, she wasn't at Larry's. With all this rain about he hoped she was okay.

Kelleigh had risked everything to save his community. He wished there was some small way he could thank her. But seeing her again and having to say goodbye, knowing that it would be the last time was going to be harder than he thought. There would be no more chances of their paths ever crossing. She'd chiseled her way into his heart and made him feel things he didn't think would ever be possible again. Why was everything so temporary?

Yes ... Jessica had been right. The universe did conspire in mysterious ways, but not everything ended in a happy ever after.

Chapter 21

Kelleigh walked around her room at Harrigan's on Thursday morning in a daze, packing up all her belongings. Folding her clothes, packing her shoes and collecting her toiletries. Rolling up all her maps and gathering up her documents. Tonight would be her last night here.

The phone call she'd been expecting had happened ten minutes prior. Toru gave her the news that the development application had been rejected. He'd given her the order to pack up, clear the gear off-site and send the crew back to Melbourne. Since pulling her aside yesterday after the meeting and accusing her of undermining the project, she had no tolerance for her boss anymore. Their words had become heated when she questioned his motives behind paying off Jerry. Revealing to him she had the evidence on her phone if he didn't confess. Reluctantly Toru admitted it was all for a massive bonus and meeting corporate targets and goals. What a scumbag. Knowing Toru would suffer as well filled her with a huge sense of satisfaction.

Toward the end of their call, Toru had curtly reminded

her that under the terms of her employment, she had four weeks until she finished up at JLR. She wasn't looking forward to telling her team this morning, or looking for a new job, or traipsing through recruitment sites and attending interviews. She had no income protection to cover loss of employment. Her insurance payout from her car would hold off the banks for only a little while longer.

Sitting down on the side of her bed, she started to put on her boots to head out on-site. It was going to be a long, wet, muddy day packing up all the gear and surveying markers with her team. It would be her last day at Larry's and driving past Gumtrees. Closing her eyes, images of Troy danced behind her eyelids. She wondered if he'd heard the news yet and wondered how he'd be celebrating the win.

The TV caught her attention; she reached for the remote on the bedside table and turned the volume up. The screen flashed with flood warnings in the area, advising people not to undertake travel unless it was absolutely necessary. *Yep, getting out of here was definitely a necessity.* The creeks were up and flooding in low-lying areas was a growing concern. She jumped to her feet. *Shit!* Her team had left their large tripods and some of their surveying equipment near the creek flat on Larry's farm. It was going to be the last area they had to survey before heading home. She had to get out there as soon as possible to make sure none of the equipment was lost. She didn't need Toru accusing her of damaging and losing expensive equipment.

Driving through the rain out to Larry's for the last time, Kelleigh absorbed in her surrounds. Rain could not hide the beauty of the rolling green hills, the countless rows of grapevines or mountains in the distance. She would miss this place and the people she'd gotten to know during her brief time here. Larry, with his love of fresh pastries and a chat over a cup of tea. Grace, watching out for everybody. Nick and

Maria at Gumtrees. And then there was Troy. Every one of her muscles clenched tightly around her heart when she thought of him. What should have been a one-night stand seemed to have developed into something so much more. Something that should never have been. Something that could not be.

"Come on, snap out of it," she cursed, trying to think of something positive about heading home to Melbourne. Fran's baby was due soon, and … and—crap, that was it. She was jobless, homeless and prospectless. What a combination. Her future was like a blank sheet of paper and it was up to her what to write. It was all up to her, no ex-boyfriends or parents to influence her direction.

***

Huge puddles of water lay on the side of the road and the thick mud squelched beneath the car's tires as Kelleigh drove toward Larry's. Either side of her, the grass, the trees and the grapevines drooped under the weight of all the heavy rain. The sky was still heavily overcast as she crested the hill and headed down to the creek crossing. It seemed like so long ago since she'd broken down here in her car.

She saw a Landcruiser and two people working between the grapevines in the paddock at Gumtrees. One pushing up against the upright post of a trellis, the other ramming the ground with a crowbar. With that old Akubra hat on his head and faded blue jeans hugging his legs, she knew instantly the man closest to her with the bar in his hands was Troy. He turned toward her as the vehicle came into his view.

Butterflies swarmed in her stomach, this would be her last chance to see him. Her chance to say goodbye.

She stopped the car, got out, jumped across a large gutter of water and waded through the long wet grass into the clearing at the start of the trellises.

Troy made his way down through the vines to greet her, his eyes shining from beneath the rim of his hat.

Troy took off his leather work-gloves and tucked them into his back pocket.

"Hi," Kelleigh said as she wiped a mound of mud off her boot on the fresh grass.

"Hey. How are you?"

"Good. How are your vines doing?" They all hung limp; looking sad, sodden and soaked through as water dripped off the ends of the leaves.

He chuckled. "They've had enough rain, that's for sure. Too much more will delay harvest because the water dilutes the sugar content in the fruit. We gotta be able to pick 'em at just the right time."

"I think everyone has had enough of the rain over the past few weeks." She squished her boots around in the mud.

Troy took a step closer. "About yesterday ... at the council meeting. I tried to find you afterward but couldn't find you anywhere."

"Yeah. I needed some time to think. I found a park in town and sat under a huge willow tree for a while."

He grinned, looking down at the ground. "I know the very place. That poor old willow tree puts up with a lot." He paused. "You looked upset after the meeting; I saw Toru and you having words."

"Lucky for me, he won't be my boss for much longer. We've all been given our marching orders now the project is cancelled."

"What? You lost your job over that?"

She shrugged. "No development. No job. No other projects in the pipeline."

"I'm sorry to hear that. I truly am. But can we backtrack a bit?" He waved his finger around in a circular motion. "What was with sending me Jerry's report via email? I was far from impressed with its inaccurate data. Then, when you came in to the meeting in a fluster and presented something totally different, I was so confused. I've been trying to sort all this muddle out in my mind but nothing has become clear."

She looked away from him, wondering how to explain the craziness of the past few days. No, make that weeks. "I had my suspicions about Toru after meeting with him and Jerry. I acted on my instincts and took two lots of samples of everything for analysis. At the festival dinner I'm sure I saw Toru paying off Jerry, but I had to have more proof. I was running out of time and options. I needed the report back for Melbourne so I could compare it against Jerry's results. I sent it to you hoping you'd find something in it as well. Luckily you did. I wanted to call, but work was busy. Toru and our lawyer arrived and I never found a free moment. After having dinner with them and I got back to my room, the report from Melbourne had come through on email. I saw the discrepancies in the data and spent half the night stressing over what to do."

"You could've kept that report from Melbourne a secret. Why risk your project?"

"It's not just about the project. It's about doing the right thing and being honest. I couldn't let Toru get away with what he'd done. The consequences of developing on contaminated land are too high. Putting the health of humans at risk is not something I could live with. So, lucky for you, no golf course and no hotel." she said as she rocked on her heels.

Troy listened and adjusted his hat on his head. "I don't know how you do it, but you keep on surprising me all the time. What you did took courage."

There was that stupid flutter in her stomach again. Damn it! She had to look away.

"Yeah well, now I have to go and tell my team the news. We'll be packing up today and be heading to Melbourne tomorrow. I'd better get going before it rains again," she jutted her chin to the west, "and by the look of those clouds it won't be long before it starts." Her hand trembled as she placed it out in front of her to shake his hand goodbye. "It's been nice meeting you." Why was saying goodbye so hard ... and awkward?

Troy grabbed her hand, stepped toward her and kissed her on the cheek. She closed her eyes as moments with him over the past few weeks flashed before her. Their first night together, the walk in the gardens, the wine tasting in the cellar and the magical time at the festival dinner. Their time was up and it was time to say goodbye. Droplets of rain started to fall on her face as his lips lingered on her skin for the briefest of moments before he stepped away.

"It has been a pleasure meeting you. Most of the time anyway." He swallowed hard. "Have a safe trip home."

Her chest ached at the thought of having to turn around and leave. Why had he touched her heart so deeply in such a short span of time? She'd never believed in love at first sight, but couldn't deny how she felt for him now. So much had happened within the span of a few short weeks. What was that song ringing in her head? Was it the Roxette song from *Pretty Woman*? In this world of reality, there would be no knight in shining armor riding in on his horse to rescue her. No handsome man in his Akubra driving after her in his Landcruiser. Nope. It was time to move on.

A loud rumble crossed the sky and the rain started to fall heavier. Another wet day out in the field. At least it would be the last.

Troy's eyes swirled with concern. "The creeks are up from all this rain. If we get another couple of inches, the crossing over to Larry's will be impassable. You don't want to get stuck. Keep an eye on the weather, okay?"

"I'll keep an eye on it." She struggled to get her feet moving. "You take care." She stepped forward and kissed him on the cheek. Breathed him in one last time before she whispered goodbye, turned away and rushed back down through the paddock to her Landcruiser.

"Kelleigh—"

His voice made her heart jolt and the first tear slipped from her eyes. But she didn't turn back. She couldn't. This was hard enough. She yanked the door open, jumped in the driver's seat and sped off down the road.

Chapter 22

Troy looked out the window of his cottage across the vineyard to the road that separated Gumtrees from Larry's. He could barely make it out through the thick curtain of rain. He sipped on his afternoon cup of coffee, the steam curling up and misting in front of his face.

This morning, Kelleigh stopping to say goodbye had torn at his insides, knowing it would be the last time he'd see her. But what could he do? What would he have said if she turned back around when he called to her?

The noise of the rain on the tin roof was deafening. The torrential downpour had been getting worse for the past few hours. His concern for Kelleigh was growing. He'd seen her team leave from Larry's at noon when the rain had begun to get heavier. But he could still see her Landcruiser parked down near the creek bed in the paddock. It wasn't far from the rising waters. What was she doing?

The thought of her all covered in mud, soaking wet, and peeling her saturated clothes off of her body brought a smile to his face. But he was startled from his daydream when he heard on the radio another severe flood warning and more torrential rain was heading their way. The water would be starting to cross the road now. He'd warned her about the rising water, why wasn't Kelleigh leaving?

A sharp pain burst in his kneecap. His reflexes caused him to bend it and smacked it hard against the kitchen cabinet in the process. *Fuck!* He'd never had a shock like this in his joint before. The odd ache and grievance, but nothing ever like this. He stood up straight and glanced back down toward the creek crossing. His stomach twisted into knots like a ball of bailing twine. Something wasn't right. He grabbed his keys off the table, his oilskin coat and Akubra and headed out the door. Splashing through the mud, he jumped in his Landcruiser, headed down the driveway and up the road to Larry's.

The windscreen wipers slid noisily back and forth across the windscreen, squeaking with each wipe. The teeming rain made it hard to see as he approached the creek crossing. He was right. The water level had risen drastically. He wound down the window to look at the swarming mass of water making its way down the Valley. The serene creek had transformed into a raging rapid before him. The rickety old concrete bridge was nearly a foot under water.

"Help!" The piercing scream sliced through the air and speared the center of his chest.

Kelleigh!

His eyes darted toward the direction of the voice. He scanned up and down the creek bank, looking in among the fallen trees and long overgrown grass.

"Kelleigh?" he yelled as he jumped out of the car and dashed along the edge. "Kelleigh?"

"Troy!"

There, he saw a flash of bright orange. The sleeve of her hi-vis shirt. As he got closer he saw her on the other side stuck in an old fallen tree. The water swirling around her waistline.

"I'm stuck. My foot. I can't it get out. Help me, please!"

The terror in her eyes and tremor in her voice sent panic through his system. The tree was huge. The water level was rising quickly. How was he going to get across to her without risking his own life?

"Are you hurt?"

"My foot. It's twisted and stuck in the tree. I can't get it out." Tears streamed down her face as she tried to pull her leg free. She winced in pain as she cried out. "Troy, help! Get me out of here!"

"I'm coming!" With that, he dashed back up to his Landcruiser and kicked the engine to life. Without a moment's hesitation he headed for the swollen creek to cross the bridge.

Shifting the gear stick into low-range, he motored through the stream. The waters parted as the work ute charged on through. The water wasn't too high yet, only just below the top rim of his wheels. The engine purred its way over the bridge. Safely across the other side, he jumped out of the car, grabbed fence pliers from his toolbox and ran over to cut the fence. Driving all the way up to Larry's house and then down through the paddock would take too much time. Time he didn't have. He had to save Kelleigh.

With four loud snaps, Troy cut the rusty wires and threw each strand out of the way for him to drive through. Jumping back into the cabin, he charged the car up the embankment and into the muddy terrain, heading straight toward Kelleigh.

"Hurry, please!" He heard her desperate cries as he grabbed the crowbar out of the Landcruiser's tray and dashed down to the water's edge. He waded through thigh-high water to reach her. "What happened?" he yelled over the rushing water.

"I was trying to walk across this to the embankment to retrieve some of the surveying equipment. Hurry! The water.

It's rising too fast."

"Do you think your foot's broken?" The rain soaked him through, trickles running off the brim of his hat and down his back.

"No, it's fallen through a rotten piece of timber, and something has lodged over the top of my foot. I can't get it off. I can't get my boot off. I'm stuck. Please hurry."

The water swirled around her. He tried not to panic as the water crept higher and higher. The current getting stronger and stronger.

Troy leaned down and felt the log underneath the muddy water. He couldn't see anything so he had to feel the shape of the log, judge where Kelleigh's foot was and work out how the hell he was going to get her out.

"Okay, I'm going to try and smash the trunk near the top of your foot. If's it rotten it shouldn't be too hard. I don't want to hurt you."

She bit her lip and nodded. Her red cheeks were flooded with tears, interlaced with the pouring rain.

Troy stood up with the water swirling around his legs, assured his footing was secure and raised the heavy metal bar up in front of him. He brought it down onto the log beneath the water. A dull thud sounded in his ears. Kelleigh winced as no doubt the vibrations coursed up through her leg.

Troy hit the spot several more times before he stopped. He leaned down and felt the wood beneath the surface of the water to see how he was progressing. God, he'd hardly made a dint. Damn hardwood.

Kelleigh tried to dislodge her foot and started to whimper. "It's still stuck."

All he could do was raise the crowbar and try again.

"Hit it harder. Hurry."

"I am. I don't want to break your foot."

"Don't worry about my fucking foot. I've got steel-caps on. Get me out of here. I don't want to drown."

The anguish and panic in her voice made him fight his own fears. *Come on!* He coaxed himself. This wasn't Nicola who always toyed with death; this was Kelleigh. She was begging to live and desperate for life. It tugged at his heart, making him fight harder to free her.

Troy started to sweat as he pummeled at the log again. The water was hindering the hard blows. Of all the trees to be stuck in, she had to pick a hardwood.

As the water reached their waistlines, he was running out of options. There was no time to do anything else. No time to call for extra help. This had to work. Kelleigh sat on the log in the water; her eyes were closed and tears rushed down her cheeks. Strands of her hair stuck to her face; her lips were trembling and turning blue. She looked like an angel praying, saying her last words, but Troy was adamant heaven wasn't going to take her yet. God was going to have to wait. With grit and determination, Troy heaved the bar above his head and brought it down with such force, the reverberations ricocheted up his arms.

He gasped as the wood finally split. With three more mighty blows the tree broke. Wading down beside her, he felt the hole he'd made in the stump and pulled the broken timber away. Reaching in with his hands, he cleared away the debris and dislodged a chunk of wood to free Kelleigh's foot.

He caught her in his arms as she fainted. Scooping her up quickly, he made his way back to the Landcruiser. Placing her in the passenger seat, he rested her head carefully against the side of the cabin and wrapped her in his oilskin coat.

He threw the crowbar in the back, rushed around to the driver's seat and headed back through the paddock. The water had risen a foot higher since he came over the bridge and the flow was now too dangerous to cross. With access to Larry and

Brian's house cut off from the floodwaters too, he only had one option. He turned the car up the road, entered through a side access gate into Gumtrees, crossed over the top ridge paddock and back down along the far road. Thank God for four-wheel drives. It was a long way around back to his cottage, but he needed to get Kelleigh safe and warm.

Chapter 23

Twenty minutes later Troy pulled up outside his cottage, rain still bucketing down from the heavens. He darted around to the passenger side of the Landcruiser, opened the door carefully and caught Kelleigh in his arms. When fresh raindrops splattered onto her face she finally stirred as he carried her inside.

"You're okay, Kel. I've got you. I've brought you back to my place. You're safe now."

Holding her close to his chest, her shivering body had him head straight for the bathroom. He placed her gently down on top of the closed toilet seat and made sure she had her balance.

"Can you sit upright while I get the shower running? You need to get out of these wet clothes and warm up as soon as possible."

She nodded, as her pale blue lips trembled. Her green eyes watched his every move as he opened the glass door of the shower and turned the taps on. Once the temperature was right, he came back out and knelt in front of her.

The muddy trail of water he'd brought into his house could be mopped up later, his only concern now was for Kelleigh. He grabbed her good foot, unlaced her boot and took it and her saturated sock off. Then he reached for the foot that had been caught. He rolled up her wet workpants and carefully removed the lace from her boot. She let out a pained cry as he slid it off her foot and peeled the sock away.

He winced when he saw the flaming redness, the scratches and the bruising starting to swell across the bridge of her foot. "Are you sure it's not broken?"

"I'm sure. Look. I can wiggle my toes." He watched her move her soft-pink nail-polished toes up and down, but the pain on her face was evident.

"Okay then. Are you right to shower, or do you need some help?"

He was stupid to think it, but he was sure he saw a flash of mischievousness in her eyes. He didn't mean he wanted to shower with her. She was hurt and cold and needed to get cleaned up so he could tend to her foot. This was no time for games. "Come on, you're shivering."

"Can you help me out of my clothes, please? My fingers are too sore from trying to free my leg." She held out her bleeding, scratched fingernails; her hands trembled profusely.

With filthy water dripping all over the floor, fending off his own chills, he stood up in front of her and offered out his hands. He pulled her to her feet, her face stopping inches away from his. Her eyes locked on to his. Her breath, warm on his face. Her body, so close to his. This was not the time to lose focus.

Kelleigh stood with all her weight on one leg, resting her sore foot on top of her other. Troy let go of her hands and started undoing her top button. His fingers fumbled as the first one popped free to reveal her flesh beneath. His eyes never left hers as he undid her shirt down to the very last button. Grabbing a handful of the fabric near her collarbones, he slipped the shirt back off her shoulders and threw the muddy attire into the basin. He was sure he detected a small grin playing at the corner of her mouth.

He dropped his gaze to the top of her work trousers, trying not to notice the gentle mound of her breasts protruding from within her now muddy-colored bra. He grasped hold of her belt, yanked the buckle free and unzipped her pants. He was going to lose his mind doing this to her. He was trying to be gentle so he didn't hurt her. Trying not to rush so she wouldn't faint again. Trying to keep his body reactions under control and avoid the swell in his pants from growing further.

He dropped to his knees and inched the fabric down her legs that clung like glue to her skin. Sitting her down again, he slipped her pants off over her feet. Discarding the trousers into the sink, he sat on his haunches before her. He was far from blind and had to admire her shapely legs, her gorgeous skin and her perfect breasts gently rising and falling with each breath. Even her bright-colored panties were cute.

He wanted to touch her all over and make sure every inch of her was all right. But the musty stench of the creek mud drew him into line. He stood and pulled her to her feet and helped her hobble over into the shower.

"Can you lift me over the base, please?"

He curled his arm around her waist and hoisted her into the cubicle. As he placed her down, she lost her balance and he stumbled in behind her. Gripping on to her tightly so she wouldn't fall, the steaming water splashed in to his face.

She placed her hands against the wall for support before hobbling around on her foot and finding her own balance. "Sorry about that."

He was about to get out when her hand caught him on the arm. "How can I ever thank you for saving my life?"

Her eyes glassed over with tears. Kelleigh leaving was one thing, but her drowning would have been horrific.

"You have to thank my dodgy knee. It's like my own form of intuition and it has a way of telling me when something's wrong. It's been working in overdrive since you came to town."

"Can I thank you, instead of your knee?" She leaned in toward him and touched her lips to his.

Steam shot up around him as her arms weaved around his neck, drawing him closer in to her. No, this was all wrong. She needed to clean up and get warm so he could tend to her foot. His eyebrows furrowed as he resisted the overwhelming temptation to respond to her kiss.

"Kelleigh. No." He avoided the disappointment in her eyes. "You need to shower and I'll tend to your foot when you're done." But as he went to exit, she put her hand over his.

Troy swallowed hard. A lump lodged in his throat. He had to leave. But she grabbed onto the front of his shirt and tugged him back into the warm flow of water and curled her arms around his neck. "Don't go. I was so frightened I was going to drown. Please stay with me." The pleading look in her eyes tugged hard on his heart.

"But you're hurt."

She drew him in closer and whispered into his ear. "I don't want to be alone right now. Please stay with me." Her soft lips kissed across his cheek before finding his lips once again. Heat shivered across his skin with each and every one of her hot breaths.

Her hands drifted down his back and her fingers felt for the bottom of his shirt. It was saturated and heavy, so he pulled back from her lips, yanked it off over his head and threw it out of the way. Pressing his body against hers, he relished the feel of skin on skin as the warm water cascaded down over them. Drifting his hands around her back, he found the clasp of her bra and eased the straps away from her shoulders.

"You're so good at that."

"Why, thank you." He grinned, admiring her naked hardened nipples. Her body was so beautiful, something so easy to adore.

Inching his hands down the side of her body, over the gentle curve of her hips, he found the top of her panties, eased them off her bottom, her legs, and freed them over her feet.

"How's your foot?" He saw the swelling was getting worse.

"What foot?"

He gazed up at her. She was beautiful. But she was injured and he had to get her off this foot.

He stood up, reached for the door and jumped out of the shower.

"Why are you getting out?" Kelleigh's voice sounded desperate and full of anxiety.

"Just getting rid of my jeans." With much effort, he clambered out of his saturated clothes and left them on top of the pile in the basin.

She smiled when he opened the door and climbed back into the shower. There was no way he could hide the effect she had on his body. She reached for him, wrapped her arms around his waist and drew him in for a kiss. With more self-control than he thought he possessed, one peck was all he gave her before he reached up into the shower caddy and grabbed his shampoo.

"What are you doing?" she asked as he squished the liquid into his hand.

"It's time for you to get washed and to bed. You need to get off that foot of yours and rest. Now, turn around so I can wash all the mud out of your hair."

Slowly she turned her back to him and let him lather her hair and soap her all over, cleaning her from head to toe. Gone was the smell of dirt and mud, now the air was filled with the scent of fresh shampoo, soap and bubbles. As he bathed himself quickly, she stood with her eyes shut, enjoying the stream of fresh water gush across her skin. But she looked exhausted.

Who wouldn't be after such an ordeal? Time to get her to bed for rest.

He jumped out of the water; towel-dried off quickly and darted out to the linen cupboard before returning with two fresh towels for her. She turned off the tap and let him wrap a towel around her, lift her out of the shower and place her gently on the mat.

Grabbing the second towel off the basin, he handed it to her. She rubbed her hair dry, then twisted the towel around up on top of her head.

Before she could argue, he grabbed her up in his arms, carried her down the short hallway and into his bedroom. Placing her down gently on his bed, he ensured she was comfortable and placed a pillow under her foot to prop it up. Then he walked over to his drawers, opened one up and started rummaging around.

"Here. Will this do?" He held up a red shirt and a black pair of drawstring sports shorts for her approval.

"They'll be fine." She took the clothes from him, discarded her towels and slipped the shirt on over her head.

Seeing her lying in his bed and wearing his clothes was playing with his head. "I'll go and grab that first-aid kit so I can bandage your foot."

"Okay," she whispered as he dashed out of the room.

*****

Kelleigh's eyes had not been able to divert from Troy as he started to head out of his bedroom. He briefly stopped at his drawers, grabbed out a pair of boxer shorts and let his towel fall away before he slipped them on.

When he disappeared out of sight, she adjusted herself to get more comfortable, wincing from the pain that shot through her foot. Once it subsided, she opened her eyes and took in her surrounds. Troy's cottage. It was the first time she'd been in here. Lying in his king-sized bed in the center of the room, she ran her fingertips over the top of his green and navy blue tartan quilt. The pillows beneath her head smelt divinely of him. Around the room it was adorned by the basics. Dark wooden bedside tables, matching drawers, a wardrobe and a few faded paintings of mountains were hung up on the walls.

The rain continued to fall relentlessly outside, pummeling against the tin roof, overflowing the gutters and the tank she could see outside his window. Staring at the rain falling, the shock and reality of what had happened kicked in. Draping her arm over her eyes, tears swelled in her eyes. She was lucky to be alive.

She pulled herself together and sat up against the headboard when she heard Troy's loud footsteps on the wooden floor and he returned with a first-aid kit.

"Let's get this all fixed up," he said as he sat on the edge of the bed next to her foot and examined it closely. "It's going to be sore and swollen for a couple of days." Taking out some ointment, he squished it over the bad grazes and scratches. She flinched as the cream stung her skin, like she'd walked through a field of nettles. "All the creeks are flooded and the roads into town are cut off. I can't get you to the doctor's until the water drops. Looks like you're stuck here for the time being."

Minutes later, he had her injured foot all bandaged up and the antiseptic cream had started to numb the pain. "All done." He packed away the kit and threw it on top of his drawers.

Unable to keep her tears at bay, they started trickling down her cheeks.

Troy rushed to her side, and sat. "What's wrong?"

"I was so scared I was going to die."

"Shh." He drew her into a hug. "It's all over now. Everything's going to be fine. Get some rest and you'll feel a whole lot better."

He kissed her on her forehead and was about to stand, but she reached out to stop him from leaving.

"Please don't go. Would you lie here next to me until I fall asleep?"

He glanced down at her hand resting on his arm. "Sure, I can do that."

He walked around to the other side of the bed and crawled on to the mattress next to her. She was only expecting him to lie with her, but he drew her into his arms and held her close to his chest. He stroked her damp hair as she listened to the soft thudding sound of his heart.

Running her hands over his firm pecs, she watched the gentle rise and fall of his chest as he took each breath. Closing her eyes, she leaned into him and kissed him softly on the side of his neck. Feeling his warmth and savoring his embrace.

Having his hot skin beneath her fingertips tempted her more and she started to explore. Tickling across his stomach, stroking up and down along his arms and trailing back across his chest. With every inch she covered, her pulse went up a notch.

She edged closer to him, kissing him lightly and blowing her warm breath into his ear. At the same time, her hand snaked toward the top edge of his boxer shorts.

His hand grasped on to hers and stopped her from going any further. He turned to face her. "What are you doing?" His sapphire eyes were dark with desire, like the storm clouds outside, high up in the skies above.

"Making sure I'm alive."

"You've just had a traumatic experience. You need to rest."

"I can't. Not yet." She reached up and touched his cheek. "I need to feel alive. Can't you tell how much I want you right now?"

"If it's half as bad as I want you, then you're in trouble," he whispered into her ear, sending goose bumps down her arm.

Troy threaded his hand up through her hair and kissed her. Kissed her so hard it took her breath away as he rolled her on to her back. Sitting up, he discarded their clothes before returning naked to her side.

He took one of her nipples in his mouth. He sucked it, licked it and tasted it as he fondled the other. Hearing him moan softly as he touched her with his tongue sent shivers to the end of every nerve.

Tousling her fingers through his hair, she giggled. No one had ever seemed to enjoy her body as much as he did. She loved his touch. Loved him feeling her. Tickling her. Tasting her.

But she wanted him inside her. Wanted to feel his weight press down on top of her. Wanted his skin flush against hers.

She tugged on his hair and drew him back to her lips. She let his weight fall across her and wrapped her good leg around his.

She gasped as he slipped his rock-hard penis inside her, sending electric shocks up along the length of her spine. She curled her toes as he started to thrust. She clenched her teeth to prevent herself from calling out in pain from hurting her bad foot, not because of any wrongdoing from Troy.

As their bodies connected, her hips pulsed against his. Every inch of his shaft penetrated her deeply as they moved together. His hot breath danced across her skin. His lips seared against hers and his gaze scorched itself into her memory forever.

Her breath quickened, her hands gripped onto his hips and his thighs tensed between her legs as he plunged harder and deeper into her. Closing her eyes, she laughed, she cried and called out his name as he sent her over the edge. He thrust into her again, releasing himself inside. The smile that inched across his face filled her heart with ... what?

Oh yes, she was glad to be alive.

Troy had done more for her in four weeks than any other man had done for her throughout her entire life. He'd helped her, stood up for her, showed her respect, made love to her, and now saved her life. She owed him everything, but had nothing to give. As she felt his breath on her neck she fought back the tears in her eyes. She'd fallen in love with him. Head over heels in love. How was she going to stop her heart from breaking when she left here, when the floodwaters receded?

As he rolled beside her and drew her into his arms, he kissed her lips tenderly. Then her cheeks. Then her forehead. Then her lips again. He smiled as he entwined his fingers with hers in front of his heart.

"I'm quite convinced you're alive." He grinned. "But it's getting late, how about I go and cook you some dinner before you go to sleep."

She nodded. "That sounds nice."

"Would you like to stay here or come out and watch TV?"

"TV. There's no way I'll be able to sleep after what we just did."

With a sparkle in his eye, he crawled out of bed. After they both re-dressed, he picked her up in his arms and took her out to the couch and handed her the TV remote.

"Is there anything you don't eat? How do lamb chops and vegies sound?"

A man who liked his meat and veg ... nice! She wouldn't have expected anything less.

"I eat nearly anything except peas," she said, screwing up her nose.

He chuckled. "I have to agree with you wholeheartedly. Those little things should be banned. You won't ever find them in my house." He kissed her on the forehead before he scuttled off into the kitchen. The sound of cupboards opening and shutting, cutlery clinking and pots and pans clanking brought a smile to her face as she hugged her arms around herself. It had been weeks since she'd had a home-cooked meal. The smells starting to come from the kitchen were promising something good.

As she clicked on the TV, her eyes wandered about the tiny room. She was sure that his quaint tongue and groove worker's cottage was smaller than her apartment in Melbourne. The sofas she sat on nearly filled the majority of the living room. With her foot propped up on the coffee table in front of her, she was sure that if she could flex her toe, she'd be able to hit the power button on the front of the small flat screen TV. Folded newspapers and wine magazines were stacked into a pile, six-inches high next to her foot. On one wall of the room, a bookshelf towered up high, half full of books and half full of trinkets—a trophy, some photos, a dozen wine glasses of mismatched sizes and bottles of liquor.

The tiny kitchen lay through a small doorway to her right, the entrance was behind her and the bathroom and two bedrooms were down the short hallway.

Muddy footprints and mess left marks on the dark timber floor from Troy carrying her in before. After dinner she'd help him clean up. With the aging pale-blue walls surrounding her, the tin roof above keeping her dry and the ancient light fittings hanging from the ceiling, Kelleigh fell in love with the old cottage. But it definitely lacked a female's touch. There were no cushions on the couch. No decorative pictures on the wall. No flowers. No bright colors. The simplicity of it all was calming and peaceful. Just Troy.

Seeing this part of him completed the memories she would be able to treasure when she went back to home.

It had been a long, emotional day. After dinner she melted into Troy's side as he sat with his arm around her shoulders and watched the news. It was just shy of eight o'clock when her eyelids grew heavy. The rhythmic sound of the rain on the roof was lulling her toward sleep. The last thing she remembered was Troy scooping her up in his arms and carrying her to bed.

Chapter 24

Troy opened his eyes and blinked a few times to focus on the vision before him. Kelleigh lay on her side next to him, sound asleep, with her golden hair fanned out across the pillow. Her long eyelashes brushed softly against her skin and he wondered what she was dreaming about. He'd had a restless night. Too many dreams and nightmares kept filtering through his mind.

The good dreams involved waking up next to her like this every morning, seeing her smile when she opened her eyes and making love to her as the sun snuck in through the curtains. Seeing her laugh, hugging her, kissing her and spending endless days together. But the nightmares jerked him from his slumber. Reliving the close call of her nearly drowning, seeing the terrified look on her face and risking his own life to save her.

He rolled on to his back and stared at the fan on the ceiling. Being with Kelleigh had stirred up so many long-forgotten feelings within such a short span of time. She'd inched her way into his heart and had him questioning everything. How had he let this happen? But it didn't matter. In a day or two, once the rain stopped, she'd be gone. He'd get over her. With a sigh, he wiped his hand over his face and rubbed his eyes. It was time to face the day. Not wanting to disturb her sleep, he slipped carefully out from under the bedsheet, headed to the kitchen and put the kettle on.

After putting Kelleigh to bed last night, he'd washed the dishes and put everything away. He did a load of washing of all their muddy clothes and put them in the dryer. He'd mopped up all the dirty wet footprints that led through the house and made the place look tidy and respectable. While he hadn't been expecting company, having Kelleigh stay was a good excuse to do the housework. Even after all that, he'd stayed up to one o'clock in the morning going through some new ideas for Gumtrees and making financial calculations. With a cup of coffee in hand and fresh eyes, he reviewed his figures once more. Everything looked good. Now he needed to talk to Nick.

He took a long gulp to finish his coffee and nearly choked on it when he saw Kelleigh appear in the kitchen doorway. He quickly wiped his mouth with the back of his hand. "What are you doing out of bed? You should have called out for me to come and help you get up. I was going to bring you some breakfast, but I didn't know what you liked to eat. I don't have much—toast and Weet-Bix is about it, or I could cook up some bacon and eggs."

She smiled as she hobbled over to an empty chair at the table and plonked herself down on the seat. Her hair was all messy and full of knots, her eyes were sleepy, but a gorgeous smile was drawn across her perfect lips.

"I'd love a coffee."

Troy stood up and made his way over to the kettle and poured her a cup, placing it down in front of her. "Can I get you something to eat?"

She shook her head. "Not yet. Coffee first."

"Not a morning person, hey?"

Troy jumped when Kelleigh took a mouthful of coffee and grimaced. "I'm sorry," she looked embarrassed. "What is this? Are you trying to poison me or something?"

Mortified, Troy didn't know what was going on. Did he make the coffee too strong for her? "No. It's just coffee."

"That," Kelleigh pointed to the cup now sitting on the table that she had pushed away from her, "is not coffee. I don't mean to be rude, but instant coffee should be illegal." She tried not to laugh as she flapped her hands in front of her mouth with her tongue hanging out. Troy felt the corner of his eyes crinkle as he tried not to laugh along with her. "Quick. I need water. Something. Anything to get rid of the taste."

He leaped up and got her a fresh glass of water, followed by a juice from the fridge.

"It's all I have. We can go over to the restaurant and get a proper coffee if you like. We can have breakfast there too. Sound good?"

Her eyes pleaded. "For coffee, that would be great. If you're still offering, I'd love some Vegemite toast."

Troy nodded. "Done."

The air quickly filled with the delicious smell of toasted bread, melted butter and Vegemite. Within a few minutes, he placed a plate full of food in front of Kelleigh, who eagerly hooked in.

"I washed and dried your clothes for you last night. But otherwise I'll see if Maria's got something you can borrow to wear while you're stranded out here. I'll also grab you one of the toiletry packs we put in the cabins so you can have a toothbrush, a comb and some lotions."

"Thanks, that's very thoughtful of you. I'll wear those shorts you gave me, but I'd be grateful for another shirt." She said, nibbling on the corner of her toast. Damn, she looked so sexy.

"I'll grab you one in a few minutes, if that's all right. I've just got to finish off this before catching up with Nick today."

"This another one of your projects?" She rolled her eyes as she sipped on her juice.

"Kind of. More of an investment into the future of Gumtrees."

"So is this different to your new function room and cabins?"

"Yes, it is."

"What's this grand plan involve?"

"I want to buy Larry's place."

Kelleigh spluttered on her mouthful of juice. "You what? Can you afford to buy Larry's?" She closed her eyes, shook her head and held up her hand. "Wait, you don't have to answer that."

After everything she'd been through with her ex and her boss, he could understand why she reacted this way when it came to talking about new ventures. He wanted her to see that he was not like them.

"Yes, Gumtrees can afford it, but I can't do it without Nick and Maria's approval. We've increased our production capacity and have had significant growth in our accommodation, restaurant and wedding business. We also have a new five-year supply agreement with Somers Hotel." Thanks to his meeting with Nate. "We're very comfortable financially. Buying Larry's makes good sense. Maintaining it as a farm provides us with instant revenue; it can supply our business with all its produce, which lowers our costs, and some of the land is ideal for growing grapes. Being able to keep it as prime farmland is what we wanted to achieve."

Her brow furrowed deeply. Here he was rattling on and getting excited about his future when she had some struggles ahead. He wished he could help her and take her worries away. He sifted through his mind; he knew many people in his line of work, but none would have the requirement to employ an engineer or project leader and none were located in Melbourne.

She reached forward and grabbed one of the pieces of paper he'd jotted down notes on. "Don't you love this stage of a project? I do. When you start trying to turn all the facts and figures and ideas from a dream into reality. All the planning and coordinating and coming up with designs. Working out in the field and developing something from scratch is so rewarding. But to be honest, after all this drama with JLR and stresses I've had with previous employers, I don't think I want to do engineering any more. Maybe it's time for a career change after all, I just have no idea what I want to do."

Troy jerked his head back. "Are you serious? I haven't known you long, but what I've seen of your work ... your presentations, your manner, your ability to manage a team, your attention to detail and trusting your instincts are all a credit to you. You have great time management skills and go beyond what is necessary for your role. You'll be an asset to anyone."

He stared at his hands on the table for a moment. *Shit.* He needed someone like Kelleigh at Gumtrees. Nick and Maria were so busy with growing business; they needed someone to help them out in coordinating all their functions. Yes, a functions manager is what they needed. He looked at Kelleigh and wondered. Nah. It was pointless; not even worth mentioning. It would be too much of a radical change, she wouldn't be interested and wanted to head on home.

"You make me believe I can do anything. Thank you for being so wonderful." She turned her head and glanced out of the small kitchen window at the rain. She looked so sad this morning. Why? What was going on? He wanted her to be happy, so it was time to distract her and get on with the day.

He reached out and touched her hand. "Come on. How about that coffee? Let's get you dressed and I'll drive you over to the restaurant. Okay?"

Kelleigh vacantly nodded as Troy set about fetching her

some clothes.

Chapter 25

Away from the noisy crowd of stranded guests having breakfast in the restaurant, Troy was having a well-brewed coffee while sitting at the counter with Kelleigh in the quiet of the cellar shop. He'd lent her his phone so she could contact her office and her team stuck at Harrigan's to let them all know she was okay. Of course, she left out all the finer details about nearly drowning.

"There you are." Maria gasped as she burst through the door and strode toward him. "I've been looking for you everywhere. Don't you answer your phone?"

Troy placed his coffee down on the wooden counter and picked his phone up from the bench. "Sorry, I had it on silent."

At the sight of Kelleigh, she hesitated and a smile spread broadly across her face. "I didn't know you had company. Here I was thinking you were slacking off work because of all the rain."

He shook his head, feeling his cheeks redden. "Nope. I've been rescuing and looking after the injured. Kelleigh got caught in the floodwaters; I got her out and am now nursing her back to health."

Maria looked down at Kelleigh's bandaged foot, nodded with a twinkle in her eye. Between her and Grace, they knew everyone's business.

"I'm glad you're safe, Kelleigh," Maria said before turning back to him. "Can you play doctors and nurses later? I'm in a dilemma. I've just got off the phone to one hysterical, stressed-out bride. Providing the creeks drop in time, her wedding with thirty guests is here tomorrow. We were supposed to have the ceremony in the gardens, but it's too wet to even put up the marquee. We can't do it in the restaurant because we need to lay it out for the reception. I've got issues with catering supplies not getting through. Staff can't get here because of the road cut-offs. I've got stranded guests to feed and entertain. On top of all that, Nick's come down with the man flu and flaked out in bed." She stopped and pressed the palm of her hand against her head. "I can't think at the moment. Where the hell can we hold the wedding service?

Maria was like a well-oiled machine when it came to coordinating everything; he'd never seen her look so flustered. "We'll come up with something." Troy sipped on his hot coffee, taking a moment to think. "What about the barn or the wine shed?"

"You can't have a wedding in a production shed around all that equipment, and the barn is filthy," Maria gasped, looking mortified at his suggestion.

"Is there a reason you can't do it in here?" Kelleigh waved her finger, indicating to the cellar shop. "It's gorgeous in here and large enough to accommodate that many people. All this beautiful timber and sandstone tiles would look wonderful with a few decorations. Have you got some candles or fairy lights, ribbons and flowers? It would make it intimate and romantic."

Troy turned and smiled at her. She was absolutely brilliant.

"That could work. All I'd have to do is roll the wine barrels out of the way, clear the displays and set up some seating. What do you think, Maria?"

"I love it." Maria beamed, clapping her hands. "Kelleigh, you're a life saver. Troy, can you fill in for Nick and do a wine tasting for the guests in here after lunch, and then I'll bring all the decorations over. If you could set them up for me, that'd be a great help too. I need to go and call the bride to put her mind at ease and get stuck into the cooking. Now the rain has stopped, let's hope the creeks drop in time and all goes to plan." Maria spun around and shot out the door as fast as she had arrived.

"You've just won Maria over. This wedding business has taken off and we can't keep up with the demand. We'll be set once the new function room is built after this coming harvest."

"Gumtrees is so beautiful, I can't believe you only recently started doing weddings here."

"We've been more of a getaway type place rather than a wedding venue. But word-of-mouth spread and now it is one of the most profitable areas of our business. So, if I have to play wedding decorator this afternoon, I need to get some work done over in the shed first. Would you like to come over and hang out or head back to the cottage?"

She seemed to deliberate for a long time on what he thought was such a simple question. "I don't want to get in your way. I'll go back to the cottage, watch TV and rest my foot. Will you come back and have lunch with me?"

Being separated from her, even if it was only for a few hours until lunchtime, seemed too long and weighed down heavily in his chest. What on earth was going on with him? He couldn't let her get to him anymore, because once those creeks dropped she was out of here. Reassuring himself, he nodded and forced a smile. "Lunch it is. Come on, let's get going."

***

Having spent enough time cooped up inside Troy's cottage, Kelleigh joined him over in the cellar shop while he did a wine tasting with a small group of six stranded guests. She sat out of the way, perched on a bar stool at the end of the timber counter and sipped on a semillon while Troy kept the wine flowing into the glasses of each guest.

Twisting her glass between her fingertips, she watched and listened to Troy as he shared his knowledge on wine, the vineyard and Gumtrees' history. The sound of his deep voice held her entranced as he spoke with heart. She wished she could be passionate like that about something.

With her head starting to buzz from the wine, and Troy's voice filling the air, images of her private wine tasting with him in the main cellar danced through her mind. His tasty lips on hers after each glass, his tantalizing hands on her as he slowly undressed her and then taking her from behind. The delicious memory would stay with her forever. This wine tasting was simply nowhere near as good in comparison.

She was pulled from her thoughts when the large wooden door opened with a gush of air. Troy held it for all the guests to tumble outside and seconds later Maria trundled in with a trolley with four large boxes strapped to it.

"Here you go," she said, standing the trolley upright. "These are all the wedding decorations for you to put up, please. I'll leave it in your very capable hands to make this room look spectacular."

Troy mumbled under his breath and Kelleigh giggled, topping up her glass with wine from the bottle Troy had left her with.

"Please let me know when you're done. I have a list as long as the Nullabor Highway to get through, so I'll catch up with you later. Thanks for this. You're a treasure." Maria patted Troy on the side of his face before rushing off out the door.

As the door clicked closed behind her, silence took over the room. Alone with Troy again.

He sighed heavily. "A man's work is never done," he said as he started to unload the boxes off the trolley and opened up each one. "Shit, look at all this stuff. Fairy lights. Material. Ribbons. What the hell am I supposed to do with all this?"

"You want me to help?" Kelleigh offered. "I love setting up party decorations. Come on, this will be fun."

"I doubt it," Troy walked over to the center of the room and grabbed one of the wine barrels that was used as a bar table, tipped it sideways on to its rim, and rolled it toward the far end of the room.

Kelleigh tilted her head to the side. Biting down hard on her lip as she watched his strong arms flex as he rolled the barrel along.

"You right there?" His sapphire eyes flashed in her direction.

She blinked, heat flushing her cheeks.

"Okay, you want to help?" he asked, planting his hands on his hips. Kelleigh nodded. "Could you work out something to do with all that," he pointed to the boxes of decorations, "while I clear away the rest of the barrels?"

"Sure." She slid down off the stool, being careful of her sore foot, but he found her eyes drifting back toward his backside as he moved the next barrel.

"Kelleigh," he called out to her from the other end of the room.

"Mmm."

"You're going to have to stop watching my ass or we won't get anything done in here."

"I was just admiring the view." She sculled the rest of her drink and turned her attention to the boxes of decorations.

"You're so bad," he chuckled. "I'll just go and a grab a ladder, hammer and nails to put up some of those lights."

***

After sorting through the boxes and formulating a plan on how to decorate the room, Kelleigh went about directing Troy on where to hang up the fairy lights. As she sat on one of the bar stools untangling the next strand of lights, she fantasized about the idea of one day having a wedding. A vineyard would be such a romantic setting. The natural surroundings, wine, photos among the trellises, the gorgeous sunsets and luxurious accommodation to retreat to at the end of the night. It sounded like the perfect day. But for her, there was nothing like that in her foreseeable future. Not even a man. Finding one to make her feel like Troy did was going to be a challenge.

She looked up at him as he struggled to nail a set of lights to the beam.

"Can I ask you something?" she asked while continuing to unravel the strand.

"Sure. Anything." He shifted the ladder along to the next beam.

"How come you never remarried?"

He hesitated as he put his foot up on the first step, fumbled with the lights, before he continued up the rungs. "I guess I've never met the right woman."

"I can't believe you haven't found someone else to share your life with. Are you still hung up on your wife? Is that it?"

Kelleigh nearly dropped her decorations when she saw pain inch across his face. "No. Nicola died a long time ago. That's not the reason at all." He hammered a nail into the wooden beam with force. She didn't want him to be defensive or make him uncomfortable, but she sensed he had the capability to love someone, but was afraid to do so.

"What was she like? Your wife? Can you talk about her?"

"Why do you want to know this stuff?" He hooked the lights over the nail and climbed down the ladder. "It's all in the past. I've moved on with work here at Gumtrees and getting to know my son." With his unsteady voice, was he trying to convince himself?

"You loved her a lot, didn't you?" She could see it written clearly on his face.

"Yes, I did." He eased himself down to sit on the bottom rung of the ladder.

"Is she the reason you've never been in love again?" She closed her eyes, trying to keep her own feelings for him at bay. She wasn't sure she wanted to hear his answer.

He scratched at the stubble on his cheek. The look in his eyes made her heart ache. "Maybe ... we met when I was seventeen, just after I'd gone to the States. We got married when we were twenty-one and after that things started to change." He hesitated as he stared down at some point on the tiled floor. "She grew very ill. She suffered severe depression and mental health issues after living through her childhood with an abusive father. I did everything I could to help her, but it was never enough. I don't want to risk losing someone I love like that again."

She found it hard to swallow as he talked. Seeing the anguish on his face was heartbreaking. It broke her own heart at the same time, knowing he didn't feel that way about her.

"What if someone came along unexpectedly and turned your world upside down?" Like he had done to her.

"This place is my world. I don't have time for anything else."

Her heart lurched inside her chest. Had he really developed no feelings for her in the time they'd been together? How did men do that? Sleep with someone ... several times ... and remain emotionally unconnected. Goddamn it! She got herself into this mess; she had to get herself out of it. One day, if she was lucky, she'd find someone who loved her as much as he loved Nicola.

"Fair enough." She looked up to the ceiling. She took several long deep breaths to regain her composure and stop the tears from stinging her eyes. She was a fool to think there was a remote possibility that Troy liked her as much as she liked him. An utter, utter fool. The sooner she could leave Gumtrees the better. "Well, these decorations aren't going to hang themselves, let's get on with it."

***

After two and half hours of hanging up hundreds of fairy lights across the wooden beams, laying out chairs, dressing them with covers and ribbons and decorating the benchtops, it was done. Troy sat on the floor, leaning back against the wine barrels at the back of the room next to Kelleigh as they looked up at all their handiwork. The fairy lights twinkled up above and filled the room with a soft ambient light. He chinked his glass against hers. "To a job well done. There's no way I would have ever made the room look this good without your help."

"It was fun."

"You're a natural," he said. "Maybe this could be your new calling. Party decorating extraordinaire."

She laughed. "You did all the work. I supervised."

Kelleigh winced in pain , moving to straighten out her leg.

"How's your foot after all the hobbling around?"

"Sore. I'm concerned about being able to drive, but I don't want to be a burden on you. If the creeks are down tomorrow, can you give me a lift back over to Larry's to get my car? I'm sure I'll be able to make it back to Harrigan's from there."

"I can do that." He reached for the bottle of semillon and

topped up their glasses once more. "Have you had enough of me already and want to leave?"

She shook her head, her eyes turned downward. "Far from it."

He watched her lips as she touched the glass to her mouth and took a sip of wine. Damn, she was so sexy. He closed his eyes and leaned his head back against the hard wood of the barrel.

"You okay?" she asked, placing her hand on his thigh.

"Yeah, I was thinking about what a crazy couple of weeks it's been since you came to town."

He turned toward her to find her gazing at him. She tucked her hair behind her ear and smiled. She was so beautiful.

"We've had a bit of fun, haven't we?"

Whether it was the few glasses of wine swirling through his insides or the magic setting she helped to decorate, or just being in her presence, he wanted to kiss her. Heat surged through his veins as he leaned in toward her and edged his mouth closer to hers. His skin tingled when she rubbed her hand slowly up and down along his thigh. Barely two inches from her mouth, he paused and breathed in her scent, filling up every one of his senses. "I'll be sorry to see you go."

Her breath quickened as his own heartbeat thudded in his chest. He closed the gap between them, his lips connected to hers at last. Tasting her top lip, then her bottom lip, and every element of her mouth.

He snapped back away from her when the door opened with a loud bang and Maria backed her way inside carrying a tray laden with hot, steaming food. Her eyes spun toward him sitting next to Kelleigh, and looked horrified for interrupting.

"Oh crap! I'm sorry for barging in. When you hadn't come in for dinner, I thought you were still in here working. Not ... not ... you know."

Trying to hide his embarrassment, Troy ruffled his hands through his hair and glanced at Kelleigh. She blushed while fumbling her hands and fingers together on her lap.

"I'll leave this here for you." Maria walked over to the bar and placed the tray of food down before she looked up around the room. "Wow. This place looks amazing. Troy, please tell me you did not do this, otherwise you have a hidden talent that we'll need to exploit further."

"No," he shook his head. "It was all Kelleigh. She ordered me around and told me where to put everything."

"It's brilliant. I think we're going to have one very happy bride tomorrow."

"I'm glad I could help out." Kelleigh looked humbled.

"Anyway," Maria dusted her hands off on her cooking apron, "I have cakes in the oven so I'll leave you two alone. Sorry for the interruption." Her grin was as wide as the Cheshire cat's as she turned and scuttled out the door.

"We can't let hot food go to waste." Troy stood up, grabbed the tray of food, along with another bottle of wine, before returning to the floor. His belly grumbled as he surveyed the hot dishes of rice, beef stroganoff and home-baked bread. He handed Kelleigh a fork and they tucked into the meal.

Seeing her glow as she enjoyed her food filled him with inner warmth. Her smile caused strange sensations to swirl inside his belly. Her laughter rippled through him and made his heart thump like the *thud, thud, thud* from a subwoofer. He thought he'd never be capable of ever having feelings like this for another woman again. Her leaving tomorrow was tearing him up inside. He would miss her but they just weren't meant to be.

After finishing off the bottle of wine, Troy scooped Kelleigh up in his arms and drove her back over to his cottage. She was giggly, bordering on tipsy, and had trouble standing as he helped her through the doorway and on to the couch. He laid her down gently, slipped off her boot and socks, before he realized she'd fallen asleep. Crouching down beside her, he brushed her hair back away from her eyes and stared at her. Saying goodbye tomorrow was going to be difficult. He leaned forward and kissed her on her forehead before he whisked her up into his arms, carried her to his bed and tucked her in for a good night's sleep.

Chapter 26

With the floodwaters receded, a wedding on and field work to do, today was going to be a hectic Saturday at Gumtrees. Troy strolled into Nick's office with his laptop, a pile of notes tucked under one arm and a cup of steaming coffee in the other, ready for a quick catch up before the day got underway. Maria was already seated at the small meeting table with her own notes and list of things to discuss.

"Where's Nick?" Troy asked as he took his seat.

"Coming. He's just over in the shed and will be here in five minutes or so.

"I'm so glad the creeks have dropped." Maria peered up at him from jotting down something on her notepad. "I've already had a call from the bride; she's on her way, the wedding is on and it will take place this afternoon as scheduled. Thank you for helping out yesterday afternoon and setting up. It was nice to have one less thing to worry about."

"I couldn't have done it without Kelleigh," Troy said, sipping on his coffee.

"So ... anything happen with you two last night?" Maria

asked, raising her eyebrow with interest.

"Yeah. Heaps." He grinned cheekily. "She had a bit too much to drink and passed out on the couch. Great night had by all."

"I didn't mean to walk in on you last night," Maria fiddled with her pen. "It looks like you two were getting very cozy."

"No, it was perfect timing before I did something I'd regret." He'd had too many of those in his life and wasn't about to have another. While he'd enjoyed taking care of Kelleigh last night, and having her presence filling his home was a nice change, their hours left together were numbered. "I'll have to take her over to Larry's later on today to get her car, and then she'll be out of here; off back home to Melbourne."

"That's a shame. You look good together. First time I've seen you take an interest in anyone in a long time."

"Can we not talk about this, please?"

Maria's eyes filled with disappointment. "You're into her. I can tell. Why don't you keep seeing her? You travel to Melbourne often enough."

"No ... it's not that."

"It's what then?"

"It doesn't matter how I feel for her, or not feel. Her life is in Melbourne and long-distance relationships never last."

Maria grasped his hand. "Oh sweetie, after seeing you two together last week at the festival dance, yesterday in the cellar shop and the way she looks at you all the time, I think it's too late for that. Finding love, or the chance to love, doesn't happen very often, don't be foolish and let the opportunity pass you by."

Troy closed his eyes. Maria was talking nonsense.

"I don't need anyone. I have my work here and Conner. That's all I need."

"And Conner is great, but he's a grown man. A parent's love for a child is so different from loving a partner; you know that. Life is too short; sometimes you have to take risks. I know you haven't known her for very long. I'm not saying marry the girl, just take some time out and get to know her better. See if there is something serious between the two of you."

"What kind of life can I offer her out here? I'm not leaving here and I doubt she'd leave her family and Melbourne."

Maria looked at him; he hated seeing concern in her eyes. "You will never know unless you ask."

Troy ripped his hand out from underneath Maria's when Nick appeared in the doorway.

"What's going on? Something wrong?" Nick's gaze jumped back and forth between the two of them as he took his seat.

"No. In fact, your timing is perfect," Troy said as he shuffled on his chair and ignored Maria's lingering look. Time to put Kelleigh out of his head. "I have something important I want to talk to you about first. He turned on his laptop and turned the screen to face them. He took a deep breath to settle his stomach. "Since the JLR development fell through and Larry still wants to sell, I've crunched our figures and want to discuss the possibility of us buying his place."

"What? Buy Larry's? How?" Maria and Nick's eyes widened with interest. That was a good sign; they weren't totally opposed to the idea.

"When I was looking into how to stop the JLR development, Larry gave me his account books from the past three years. The place is doing okay considering it's not run to its full potential. His asking price is in the high hundreds and I'm confident we can do it. It will be tight but not out of our reach. We want to expand the vineyard and those lower slopes on Larry's would be great to continue our coverage of semillons. We could keep Jett on to run the place, up the head of cattle and expand the crop coverage. We'd be able to supply produce for the restaurant and sell the rest to local restaurants and cafés. Here's the figures for you to look at." Troy handed them a document for each of them to review.

"But what about the function room and new cabins? That all starts after the harvest."

"Yep. All that is accounted for as well." He pointed to a section in the document.

"I never knew you to be so business-minded. You're one step ahead of me all the time lately. Day to day operations consume all of my time. But I do like the sound of this." Nick nodded as he perused the papers before him.

"It's a logical move for us. Considering we've managed to save it from being turned into a golf resort, I'd hate to see who or what comes along next. Who knows what they'll want to do to the place."

"True," Nick and Maria said together.

"If these figures look too slim for you, another alternative is we consider getting an investor. I haven't talked to them yet, but I know they'd be interested."

"Who ... oh ... you mean Jessica?" Nick rubbed the side of his cheek.

"Why not? She loves this place. Nate loves the wine. Having her and Nate behind a place like this makes good business sense."

"I'm not sure I want to give up any more ownership of Gumtrees if I don't have to. Let us take a closer look at this and talk to our accountant on Monday. You are right; Larry's would be good for us." Nick's eyes glinted with excitement. Even Maria looked keen as she flipped through the pages before her.

"Excellent." Troy leaned back in his chair. "So what's next on the agenda?"

Nick and Maria started going through their lists with him. The whole time he listened his leg jittered up and down underneath the desk. Buying Larry's excited him. The ability to expand the vineyard and have access to all that beautiful produce would be of great benefit to Gumtrees. But time was ticking by so quickly and he struggled to concentrate throughout the meeting. Kelleigh kept leaping to the forefront of his mind. He was starting to fret at having to say goodbye.

Chapter 27

Kelleigh heard a car pull up. She was sitting on the couch in Troy's cottage, flicking through one of Troy's wine magazines with her aching foot resting up on the coffee table. She wondered who it was; with a soft purring engine it certainly wasn't a Landcruiser. Within moments of the car door opening and closing, footsteps bounded up the wooden steps and the front door burst open.

"Hello," She spun around to see a young man with piercing blue eyes standing in the doorway.

"Oh, hi." Surprise lit across his face. "Where's Troy?" He looked around, stepped across the room and ducked his head into the kitchen.

"I was still asleep when he left. He had a meeting with Maria and Nick, so I assume he's over in the office."

"Right." The blond flicked his long fringe out of his face. "I'm Conner."

"Nice to meet you. I'm Kelleigh." She should have known it was Troy's son, their eyes and physiques identical. "I've been stranded here by the floodwaters and Troy's been looking after me."

"You've been staying here?" Conner said, pointing to the floor. "Why didn't you stay in one of the cabins?"

"Um … I didn't think of that." The thought never actually entered her head.

"Oh, so you and Dad—" He jerked his thumb toward the bedroom.

Kelleigh's gaze dropped to the floor, not knowing how to respond. Her discomfort dissipated when she heard Troy's Landcruiser pull up outside. "That must be him now."

Seconds later Troy walked in and handed her a takeaway cup of freshly brewed coffee. "Oh my, you're a lifesaving coffee god. Thank you." She took the cup as he winked at her. Conner stood in the kitchen doorway with his mouth hanging open.

"Hey, Conner. I wasn't expecting you this weekend. You must have left Sydney early."

"Yep. Right on dawn. I had to come out and make sure everything was okay. The floods and warnings have been all over the news. On my drive in, it looks like there's some damage to the trellises down by the creek, is that what we're going to work on today? Fixing them?"

"Later," he smiled, remaining fixed on her as she sipped and savored the coffee. "They don't look too bad. We'll straighten them tomorrow. The sun's out, so today we need to do some leafing on the shiraz. Jimmy is over in the shed waiting for me." While he was clearly speaking to Conner, having him watch her sent tingles though her insides.

"Well, I'm here to work. Let's get to it," Conner interjected.

"I'll just be a minute."

Kelleigh wriggled on the couch. Troy had just got back from his meeting, she didn't want him to leave again so soon.

Conner rolled his eyes as Troy sat down on the coffee table next to her injured foot and gently picked it up, assessing her bruising. "How's your foot this morning? It still looks terrible. Do you think you'll be able to drive today?"

"Yes, I can put weight on it. So, I guess when you're ready, can you give me a lift over to Larry's? Then, when I get back to Harrigan's, I'll sort out a flight to go home."

"You sure?" The look in his eyes and the way he was massaging her foot was making her heartbeat erratic. She looked away and nodded. She'd overstayed her welcome; it was time to go home.

"Okay then, I'll go get this boy of mine and Jimmy out working in the vineyard and be back here in an hour or so. We'll have lunch and then set off."

"Sounds good. I'll have a shower and see you soon."

Troy patted her leg, released her foot, and walked out the door with Conner. She closed her eyes tightly as the door shut behind them. Biting down hard on her lip, she fought back the tears in her eyes. It was ridiculous, but it felt like when Troy walked out the door, he took a piece of her heart with him. This place, this life and everything about Troy had touched her in a way she never thought possible. Now she had to leave it all behind.

***

"The creek flooded badly, didn't it?" Conner looked out over the vineyard toward Larry's as he shoved his hands into a set of leather work-gloves. Jimmy wandered down the row to start leafing at the opposite end.

"Hopefully that's the last of the rain for a while. The grapes don't like so much water. It's not good this close to harvest." Troy turned his attention back to the vine in front of him and started snipping at the leaves with his secateurs. "I'm glad you came up this weekend. A lot has happened over the past few weeks and I was wondering if you've been able to make up your mind about what you want to do for work."

Conner swore under his breath, unable to establish smooth rhythm and coordination for leafing. Troy grinned, knowing it took him ages to get it down to a fine art. Conner at least kept persevering. "Well ... that's why I've come out here this weekend to talk to you. If your offer is still there, I'd love to come out here and work."

Troy stopped before he snipped at another leaf and turned to face Conner. To have his son working alongside him would mean the world to him. After so many lost years, being patient and taking the time to establish a relationship with him, he couldn't ask for anything more. "Really? You mean that?"

Conner stopped pruning the leaves and scuffed his boot into the soft mud. "Yeah. I do. Since getting to know you and spending a lot of time out here, it's really grown on me. I don't want to be an architect anymore. I hate that I've wasted three years of my life on a degree I'll never use, and I know for certain I don't want to work at Pepe's Pizza for the rest of my life."

Troy took a deep breath to stop being overwhelmed. "What are you interested in? Harvest starts in two or three weeks so there's a lot of field work at the moment. We're going to expand the vineyard, so you can learn the viticulture side of things. There's equipment maintenance or landscape gardening. Winemaking. Business administration, accommodation management or the restaurant. What about being a coordinator for all the wedding business that Maria is attracting?

"Ew, definitely not functions. That sounds too much like Mum's event management business." Conner shaded his eyes as the sun finally broke through the clouds.

"So, what interests you?" he asked again.

Conner shrugged. "I want to do everything and anything outdoors. If you don't mind, I think I'd like to take on viticulture.

What you do is more like a science and I like that. Maybe there's a lot more of you in me than I realized."

Troy's knees nearly buckled beneath him. Conner was serious. He never thought he'd see the day. "You ... want to be a viticulturist? Like me? You do know its hard work. Long days, labor-intensive, hot, stinky, demanding work."

"I've worked out here enough over the past two years to have a good idea of what goes on. If you think it's necessary, I'll enroll into an agricultural management course and study part-time. You're here to teach me everything else I need to know. Moving out here is all I've thought about for months. It's not as if I'm making this choice on the spur of the moment. Becky hated it when I mentioned coming out here; that's one of the reasons we broke up. I know this is now part of my life. I just didn't know how much I wanted it until recently."

"Wow, I don't know what to say." Troy was sure his mouth was hanging wide open.

"Your DNA sucks, old man. But I can't deny I'm your offspring."

"Have you told your mother?" Oh Lord, what would Jessica say?

"Nah, I was waiting to talk to you. This is going to be so cool."

"So when do you officially want to start?" Troy took off his Akubra, wiped the sweat from his brow on his sleeve before replacing the hat on his head.

Conner stopped and thought for a moment. "How about in two or three weeks when harvest starts. I have to give notice and resign from Pepe's. Oh, wait what are you going to pay me? The wage better be more than I'm earning now. Minimum wage sucks."

Troy tried not to laugh. But more than anything he was thrilled Conner was going to come out here and work alongside him. "I'm sure we'll pay you better than that. Having you here means so much to me. It's going to be great." He put his hand out and Conner grabbed it in a firm shake before Troy drew him into a hug. This was one turn of events he never saw coming.

"Must admit though, I'm not looking forward to shacking up with you in that small cottage of yours," Conner smirked.

"Well, there may be some developments there that I will fill you in on later."

"I haven't even lived with Mum for years and suddenly living with you is going to be weird. What if I go out and want to bring a girl home?"

Troy chuckled. "I'm sure we'll work something out. Why? Are you seeing someone new already?"

"I've been texting Alice, you know, Grace's granddaughter. We met at Harrigan's the other weekend when the festival was on." Conner couldn't meet his eyes.

Troy gasped. "Isn't she only seventeen?"

"She's eighteen. And she's cute."

"Well, good luck with that. I wouldn't want to be you when Grace finds out. You'll soon discover Grace has a way of finding out everything that's going on in this place. So be warned if you aim to corrupt her one and only granddaughter."

"Thanks for the warning." Conner said as he struggled to cut a thick stem. "But maybe that's one trait I got from Mum. Her kick-ass determination. She's always told me if you want something bad enough, you gotta make it happen, regardless of the obstacles that stand in the way. So if Grace is my only issue, I'm not worried in the slightest."

Conner's wise words hit Troy fair in the solar plexus. Jessica had done a fine job raising him into a fine young man. He couldn't be more proud.

Conner flicked some flies away from buzzing around his face. "On that note, are you going to tell me about the woman who's shacked up in your cottage or not?"

"Not." Troy grinned at Conner as they continued along the vines, trimming away some of the growth from the side facing the sun to help ripen the fruit. Carefully taking hold of a stem, he tweaked away the leaves with his secateurs with speed and efficiency. "My love life, or lack thereof, is none of your business."

"It became my business when you zoned out and acted like there was no one else in the room back there. I know. It's how Mum and Nate act around each other. Not pleasant to watch on my part, but you've got it bad for her whether you admit it or not. So who is she?"

"Her name's Kelleigh and it's complicated. She's been here in town for a few weeks and we've seen each other a few times. It's no big deal."

"Right." Connor's voice drawled. "And?"

Troy shrugged. "She's leaving today; heading home to Melbourne." Troy snipped madly at a few leaves. He glanced at his watch; time was ticking away too quickly and soon he'd have to head back to the cottage to drive Kelleigh over to Larry's.

"Melbourne? That's not far. So are you going to keep seeing her?"

After Maria's suggestion this morning, he'd stewed over the possibility of a long-distance relationship, but he didn't want to only see Kelleigh on the odd getaway. When she finds work back in Melbourne, she'd probably end up working Monday to Friday, whereas he worked every weekend. The opportunity to spend time with her, if and when he visited, would always be limited. Alongside that, there'd be the long drives to Newcastle or Sydney to catch planes, wasted hours at airports and flights he wasn't fond of.

But he would see her. Be with her. Was that better than nothing?

All this turmoil rolling around in his head suddenly stopped.

It settled out before him, like sediment in the creek.

It was going to be hard. It was going to take commitment. It scared the hell out of him to take the risk, but he had to be with Kelleigh, regardless of how. But the fear of rejection and the unknown had his feet stuck in the mud. He'd survived through so much in the past and was not keen on the possibility of it happening again, but he had to find out if this crazy feeling he had for Kelleigh was mutual. They had to find a way to make it work if she felt the same.

"Yes, I'd like to. Are you okay with that?" He didn't want Kelleigh to interfere with his growing relationship with his son.

"I'm not going anywhere," Conner said. "Why are you still out here with me and Jimmy? Shouldn't you be somewhere else?"

Bracing his heart, Troy ripped off his work gloves, ran toward his Landcruiser and sped back toward his cottage.

Chapter 28

Troy's palms sweated as he gripped the steering wheel tightly on his way back to the cottage. Jumping out of his Landcruiser, he bound up the steps and kicked off his muddy boots at the door. He rushed in through the door to see Kelleigh, but his stomach dropped when he found the place empty. He checked the bedroom, the bathroom and kitchen, but she was nowhere to be found. Ripping his hands through his hair; he didn't know where else to look. Had she left already without saying goodbye?

Clenching his fist, he punched at the wall hard, but didn't leave any trace of a mark on the hardwood wall. He was too late. She'd gone. Gone without saying goodbye.

Fuck.

Shaking his hand after hurting his knuckles, he pulled out a chair at the kitchen dining table and dropped down onto the seat. Propping his elbows up on the surface of the table he buried his head into his hands.

He shook his head, trying to make sense of the thoughts pounding through his mind and tugging at his heart.

"Hey."

He jumped when her voice touched his ears. He had to close his eyes and take a deep breath to calm his heart rate down. Thank goodness, she hadn't left.

"Sorry, I didn't mean to scare you."

"I didn't hear you come in. Where've you been? I thought you might have left." He remained transfixed on her as she hobbled into the room. Doubt started to shred away his confidence and hinder what he needed to say.

"No, I went and said goodbye to Maria and Nick," she said sitting down at the table, knocking her knees against his as she pulled in the chair. "They're really nice people." She smiled, but her eyes were full of sadness. Maybe she longed to get a move on so she could head for home.

"That they are," he mumbled.

"Thank you for everything while I've been here. I don't just mean the past few days, I mean since I came to town. You've shown me that there are decent men in the world. We had our rough spots but you were always true to yourself, your friends and what you believed in. You saved my life and for that I'll be forever grateful."

"I'm glad I've left a lasting impression." He placed his hand on top of hers, feeling her soft skin.

"You certainly have," her voice barely above a whisper.

A lump lodged itself in his throat. Why was it so hard to tell her what was in his heart?

"Well!" she said, pulling her hand free and slapping her palms onto her thighs. "No point in delaying the inevitable any longer. I guess it's time to go." She stood up and the chair scraped loudly on the wooden floor.

"Oh. Right." His heart thudded abnormally in his chest. She stood behind her chair and pushed it neatly under the table. "Let's go get that Landcruiser of mine and I'll be off."

Panic set in. He couldn't let her go. Not yet. As she turned to walk out of the kitchen, he leaped from the chair, reached for her arm, spun her toward him and crushed his lips to hers. It may have been stupid, may be even desperate, but he didn't care as he pushed her back a step or two and smothered her up against the wall. His body ached for hers as her tongue danced with his. Framing her face with his hands, he kissed her. Breathed her in. Savored her touch. Relished her taste. Couldn't she tell how much she affected him? How much his heart sprang to life when she was near? He didn't realize how afraid he'd been of loving someone again until she walked into his life.

As she wrapped her arms around his shoulders, a trembling moan in her throat wrenched at his heart and he felt her tears fall against his fingertips.

No! His mind screamed. Don't let this be the last kiss. He didn't want to upset her. He squeezed his eyes shut, kissed his way along from her lips toward her ear and let the words slip from his mouth. "Stay. Stay with me."

His hands grabbed her around the hips to hold her as he felt her knees weaken.

"What did you say?"

"I don't want you to go."

"I have to."

With those three little words he felt his volatile heart shatter. Of course, she had to. What was he thinking? Stupid love. *Damn it!* He'd fallen in love with her and for what? Only to lose her. He took a step back, gutted, but nodded in understanding.

"Why do you want me to stay?" She begged him to answer while she leaned against the wall for support.

"Does it matter?"

"I need to know." She placed her hand on his chest. "Other than my sister, I have nothing waiting for me back in Melbourne. Why on earth would you want me to stay?"

"I want you to stay because you want to. There's so much work here, I could offer you a job. A place to stay. Anything you want."

Kelleigh shook her head. "For someone in my situation that sounds like a great offer, but it's not enough. I will find another job. I can crash at my sister's for a while longer. So why should I stay here? Why do *you* want me to stay?"

God, why did women always have to make everything so complicated?

He clenched and released his fists, trying to sift through emotions that felt like an elastic band about to snap. "Because if you feel for me the way I feel about you, I think you're crazy to walk away."

Her hand dropped away from his chest and another tear slipped from her eye. This was not going to plan. Not that he really had one in the first place.

"And how do you feel about me?" Her eyes were swollen with tears.

He curled his hand around the nape of her neck and pulled her lips to his. Shivers ran up his spine as he felt her body melt into his. He was lost in her. This crazy, beautiful woman had broken the lock on his heart. As he took a breath, stared into her gorgeous emerald green eyes and stroked her hair, he couldn't contain the words anymore. "I love you." He wiped away a tear droplet that fell from her eye. "Don't go because I love you and want you to stay with me."

Her lips trembled. "You love me? Really?"

All he could manage was a nod.

"I love you too." Kelleigh gushed. "Since the moment you rescued me on the side of the road. I didn't think it was possible to feel like this in such a short amount of time, but I do."

"How are we going to make this work? Will you seriously consider moving or do you want to do the long-distance thing—"

She placed her index across his lips to halt him from talking. "My life in Melbourne is over. I'd love to move here and be with you. I belong here, or anywhere, as long as it's with you."

Drawing her to him, he kissed her. With each breath, he let her into his heart. With each touch, he let her possess him. With each taste of her mouth, he let her own him. "You know," she said rubbing her hands across his shoulders, "actions speak louder than words. I really think I'd like you to show me how much you love me."

"Your wish is my command." He scooped her up in his arms and carried her down the hallway to the bedroom. She squealed in delight as he lay her down on the bed, removed her clothes and showed her just much he loved her. Kissing every inch of her body and connecting with her in every way possible.

He thought he was incapable of loving someone again. How wrong he'd been. Kelleigh may have come to the Hunter Valley with JLR to purchase Larry's property, but instead she'd acquired his heart. Forevermore, he was hers and hers alone.

Epilogue

"You ready for this?" Fran said as she handed Kelleigh her bouquet.

"Never been so ready for anything in my life." Kelleigh touched the soft petals to her nose and inhaled the sweet perfume.

"Let's do it." Fran fiddled with a flower in her hairdo once more.

Kelleigh walked over to her father, who was standing at the door waiting for her, and took his arm. Fran trotted out in front of them and led the way out of one of the cabins and down the pathway past the new function room..

"Stop fidgeting," her father whispered as they walked around the corner and into the magnificent rose garden Conner had been growing at Gumtrees. When she looked up, Troy stood at the front of the small gathering of friends and family. Suddenly, nothing else mattered when she saw him standing next to the celebrant and Conner. Not the loose strands of hair flying around her face, the alignment of her skirt, or the vail blowing in the breeze. Troy was her world. She let out a long slow breath to calm her nerves and approached the man she loved.

How life had changed in the course of nearly two years. She didn't think it was possible to love someone this much. Troy still looked at her every day like he'd done the first night they spent together at Harrigan's.

As her father placed her hand in Troy's, she knew this was where she belonged. Before the celebrant could utter a word, Troy stepped toward her and kissed her tenderly on the mouth.

The celebrant cleared his throat loudly, making Kelleigh smile.

"Dude, you're supposed to marry her first." Conner said, tugging on Troy's jacket.

The crowd before them laughed as Troy whispered, "You look so beautiful, I couldn't wait that long to kiss you. I love you so much. Now ... should we say some vows?"

"Okay," Kelleigh nodded and caught her breath.

With vows said, kisses and rings exchanged and their signature sealing the deal, she was now Mrs. Smith.

Congratulations and applause filled the air, photographs snapped and much champagne was consumed by the guests as the sun set over the lush green spring growth at Gumtrees. The evening was filled with incredible food, a lot of alcohol and plenty of dancing.

As the clock approached midnight, Troy led her onto the floor, drew her in close and moved her slowly around in time to the music. "How's my beautiful wife?"

"Deliriously happy. It's been a magical day."

"Well, I think you being a mighty fine wedding coordinator may have had something to do with it."

"Who would have thought that every weekend I get to help people's special day come true. And today I hope I made ours a memorable one as well."

"It was perfect, and now I finally get to call you my wife."

Hearing those words felt strange. He had asked her to marry him not long after she moved to the Hunter four weeks after the floods. She'd started working in the office with Maria and had dived into becoming Gumtrees new wedding and functions coordinator. She'd been adamant about clearing up all her finances before she would tie the knot with Troy. Lawyers and the police had finally tracked down Rodrigo living in Adelaide with his cousin. The courts ordered him to pay back every cent he had stolen from her. He even scored three months in jail. Her past was well and truly behind her.

Kelleigh wrapped her arms around Troy's neck and gazed into his sapphire blue eyes. "Yes you do, my handsome husband."

"Handsome." He balked. "Is that all I get? Aren't I dashing, sexy and no one else will ever compare?"

She laughed as he twirled her around the dance floor. Her head spun and she had to steady herself from feeling giddy, even though she hadn't touched a drop of alcohol.

Nate's loud cheer filled the air as Nick walked in from the bar with some of his finest vintage shiraz. "Oh no. It's going to get messy in here once Nick starts raiding the cellar." Troy glanced over to the rowdy table of guests where Nick filled glasses with wine for Nate, Jessica, Maria and a few other friends. He turned back to her. "It's getting late, want to get out of here?"

Oh yes, she was tired and wanted some alone time with her new husband. After a hectic week of family arriving, organizing the final touches for the day and getting ready, she just wanted him all to herself. With gratitude, she nodded.

Leading her by the hand, they said their goodbyes to everyone, who all desperately tried to convince them to stay.

After several minutes of farewell hugs and kisses, Troy helped Kelleigh into Conner's Audi he'd lent them, and headed off on the short drive around to their house. Her heart fluttered.

This would be the first night in their new home, up on the hills overlooking what used to be Larry's farm. It was now an extension of Gumtrees. Conner lived in the old farmhouse and their new place overlooked the Valley.

Troy parked the car outside the front door rather than in the garage, hoped out and dashed around to help her. "It's our first night in our new home; I have to do the honors and carry you across the threshold." His warm fingers entwined around her hand and assisted her out of the car. He swept her into his arms and kissed her as he carried her to the door. He swung it open, stepped inside and flicked on the lights before he placed her gently onto the ground.

"Wow. Who did this?" he said as he looked about the room.

She was stunned. Rose petals scattered everywhere and their sweet fragrance filled the room.

"I didn't do it. It must've been Maria and Conner because Fran's been with me all day. It looks amazing."

With eyes shimmering in the soft light, he shuffled closer to her and rubbed his hands up and down her arms. "You're the one who's amazing. I love you, Mrs. Smith."

"I love you, too. With all my heart."

He swooped in to kiss her, but she put her hand on his chest to stop him.

"Before we get too carried away, I have something for you." Kelleigh's heartbeat raced in her chest.

Troy furrowed his brow. "I thought our rings were our wedding present to each other. I didn't get you anything."

"They are, but this is something for the both of us. I just have to find my handbag that I dropped off here this morning. Wait here one second." She rushed into the office, scooted around all the boxes of their belongings that they hadn't unpacked yet and found her bag on the desk. Scrummaging through it, she quickly located what she needed and went back out to Troy. Her blood rushed through her veins and nausea rose in her belly. With trembling hands, she handed him the little long box.

"What's this? You bought me a pen?" Troy questioned as he took it from her.

"Just open it."

Troy fumbled with the ribbon, let it drop to the floor, and slid the box open. The breath gushed from his lungs when he saw what lay inside.

"Is this what I think it is? You're pregnant?" His eyes glistened with tears.

"I only found out two days ago and wanted to surprise you." Her voice jittered with excitement. "We're going to have a baby."

"Really? A baby?" His mouth gaped open. "I know we talked about it, but it was your decision. Oh wow, this is the best present. You've made me so happy." He curled his hand around her neck and drew her in close. "You and me, we're going to do this right. Every step of the way. I'm not going to miss one second of this. I'm not going to miss anything, like I did with Conner. You've made all my dreams come true. Thank you. Thank you so much."

She placed her hand on his cheek and wiped a tear from his cheek. "I love you." She fell into his embrace and their lips met. Lifting her once again into his arms, he headed down the hallway and into their master bedroom. With her new husband, her new house and new baby on the way, she'd finally found her home.

OTHER BOOKS BY TANIA JOYCE
visit: taniajoyce.com

THANK YOU

Thank you for reading Dangerous Acquisitions.
It would be appreciated if you could take a moment and
leave a quick review on Amazon.
https://amazon.com/author/taniajoyce

TANIA JOYCE NEWSLETTER

For staying in touch with new releases, news and events, sign
up to Tania Joyce's newsletter.
Subscribe at:
http://taniajoyce.com/newsletter/subscribe

FOLLOW TANIA JOYCE

You can follow and find Tania Joyce on the following social
media platforms.

Web: http://taniajoyce.com
Facebook: https://www.facebook.com/taniajoycebooks
Twitter: https://twitter.com/taniajoycebooks
Pinterest: https://www.pinterest.com/taniajoycebooks/
Goodreads: https://www.goodreads.com/taniajoyce
Instagram: https://www.instagram.com/taniajoycebooks/
Facebook Readers Group: https://www.facebook.com/groups/taniajoyce/
BookBub: https://www.bookbub.com/authors/tania-joyce
Amazon: https://amazon.com/author/taniajoyce